Christopher Rice published his bestselli[ng] when he was twenty-two. By thirty, Ri[ce] *Times* bestsellers, received a Lambda Literary Award and been declared one of *People* magazine's 'Sexiest Men Alive.' His noir thriller *Light Before Day* was hailed as a 'book of the year' by mega bestselling author Lee Child. His most recent book, *The Heavens Rise*, was nominated for a Bram Stoker Award.

The son of legendary author Anne Rice, he has published short fiction in the anthologies *Thriller* and *Los Angeles Noir*. His writing has been featured in the *Advocate*, the *Washington Post*, the *Los Angeles Review of Books* and on Salon.com. With his friend and co-host, Eric Shaw Quinn, Rice recently launched his own Internet radio broadcast, The Dinner Party Show (www.thedinnerpartyshow.com).

Praise for *The Heavens Rise*

'Christopher Rice is a magician. This brilliant, subtly destabilizing novel inhales wickedness and corruption and exhales delight and enchantment. Rice executes his turns, reversals, and surprises with the pace and timing of a master. *The Heavens Rise* would not let me stop reading it – that's how compelling it is'
Peter Straub

'Christopher Rice has written an amazing horror novel with more twists and turns than a mountain road. You'll think you know your destination . . . but you'll be wrong'
Charlaine Harris

THE VINES

CHRISTOPHER RICE

piatkus

PIATKUS

First published in the US in 2014 by 47North
a division of Amazon Publishing
First published in Great Britain in 2014 by Piatkus

Copyright © 2014 by Christopher Rice

The moral right of the author has been asserted.

A CIP catalogue record for this book
is available from the British Library.

ISBN 978-0-349-40286-4

Printed and bound in Great Britain by
Clays Ltd, St Ives plc

Papers used by Piatkus are from well-managed forests
and other responsible sources.

MIX
Paper from
responsible sources
FSC   FSC® C104740

For David Streets

You have taught me it's possible to keep an open heart during the most challenging periods of our lives.

BEFORE

Spring House had its portrait painted many times before it was destroyed by fire. Images of its grand, columned facade are so prevalent throughout gift shops in southern Louisiana most tourists to the region return home with a haunting sense they had visited the place, even if they didn't take a bus tour of the old plantation houses that line the banks of the Mississippi River.

Hundreds of years after the conflagration that reduced the antebellum mansion to timbers and weeds, the house and grounds were restored to a more tourist-friendly version of their original splendor by one of the wealthiest families in New Orleans. Several of the slave quarters were removed to make room for a quaint gazebo, and the cane fields where African slaves labored and died in the punishing heat were replaced by manicured, fountain-studded gardens that have since played host to countless wedding receptions. The affluent families who pay for these events feel no meaningful connection to the place's violent, bloody history; otherwise they would have second thoughts about staging such gleeful celebrations atop soil forced to absorb decades of systematic degradation and assault. No doubt, many of the brides in question grew up in homes where an etching or a painting of Spring House hung in the foyer or the upstairs hallway or, at the very least, the guest bathroom, and they too were seduced, sometimes subliminally, by these ever-present reproductions of its pastoral sprawl and muscular profile.

But there is one rendering of Spring House that continues to cause dispute among academics, and it is not found in gift shops. The sketch is primitive, but telltale architectural details of the old house are plainly visible: the widow's walk and the keyhole-shaped front door, to name a few. It depicts a gathering of slaves who have been forced to stand and watch while one of their own is whipped by a man who is clearly the overseer. The inexplicable event that seems to have interrupted the overseer's work is a matter of great contention among those devoted to the study of plantation history.

Some shape has descended from the branches of a nearby oak tree and twined itself through the overseer's airborne whip, capturing it in midair and bringing a sudden halt to the bound slave's violent punishment.

Even though it has no signature or date, the academics and tour guides believe this sketch to be the work of one of the many privileged white historians who took it upon themselves to document the personal narratives of freed slaves after the Civil War ended. Perhaps these accounts of misery moved one of these well-intentioned writers to work beyond the limits of his abilities, resulting in a crude illustration meant to manifest the sublimated rage of his interview subjects.

Or maybe it is the work of a former slave, who summoned all the steadiness of hand she could manage and put her own revenge fantasy to paper. But these scholars are sure the sketch does not depict an actual event. It's a metaphor, they insist, an angry dream spilled in ink. Of this assertion these students, who devote their lifework to studying the bloody and complex history that runs catacomb-like beneath the bus tours and the spinning racks of postcards and the five-figure weddings, are absolutely sure.

And they are wrong.

NOW

1

When she reaches the shadows at the top of the stairs, Caitlin Chaisson is stilled by the sound of a woman's drunken laughter. It comes from the guest bathroom a few paces away, where the half-open door reveals two pairs of entwined legs and a woman's hands, capped with bloodred nails, tugging a man's trousers down over his ass. She recognizes the man's pants, as well as his slurred, breathy voice, and all at once the banister on which Caitlin is attempting to rest her hand feels as vicious and hungry as a lava flow.

The last of her guests are still draining out of the foyer below, but she feels utterly alone, as if the short distance down the gentle half spiral of the perfectly restored wooden staircase is a dizzying slope, and she is perched precariously at the summit. She wants to shatter this illusion by turning and running down the stairs, by mingling once more among her guests as they retrieve their coats from the indulgent valets. After all, they are her friends, her many cousins, and employees of her late father's foundation, and they gathered that evening at Spring House to celebrate her birthday. And she's sure if she joins once more in their gin- and vodka-slurred conversations about which member of which couple is sober enough to make the long drive back to New Orleans—a serpentine crawl along winding river roads, past shadowed levees—she will be freed from the terrible implications of what she's just seen. But while the chatter coming up from the foyer below sounds bright and seductive, it is powerless to move her, as cloying and impotent as the condolence cards that poured in after the plane crash that killed her parents. So she remains frozen at the top of the stairs as her final birthday gift unfolds a few paces away.

It is the precision of what she sees next that cuts her most deeply, as if the scene had been staged for her arrival. But she knows this can't be true. The second floor of Spring House is a warren of shadows, and there are still guests sprinkled all over the long front drive, most of them following her gardener and handyman, Willie, as he leads them back to their parked cars with an antique gas lantern raised in one arm. The upstairs bathroom is the quickest escape for two people gripped by drunken lust. Worse, there is nothing calculated about the way her husband's mouth gapes against the young woman's exposed neck; rather, a blind passion animates his movements, and despite the deep, agonizing twist in her gut, Caitlin sees it for what it is: adolescent lust. But the childishness of Troy's pawing—he's almost got the woman's right breast free from her cocktail dress—does nothing to diminish its impact. It is wild and liberated in ways it has never been inside the bedroom they've shared for five years. It gives the display a terrible, crushing purity.

And the woman. Who is she? Caitlin noticed her earlier, circulating among the other guests, some yat friend of one of her cousins, she'd thought. She'd looked wide-eyed and cowed by the masterfully restored plantation house and its sprawling, manicured grounds. And yet, had she been biding her time, waiting to strike? Or worse, had this little betrayal been planned in advance? Is this not the first time her husband has twisted this delicate blonde's right nipple in between his thumb and forefinger while gnawing gently on her earlobe?

4

Caitlin is amazed they can't hear her sharp intakes of breath. She is amazed that the door is open just the right number of inches for her to see the full arc the woman's body makes when Troy lifts her up onto the edge of the sink and forces her thighs apart as much as they can go inside the confines of the dress. Caitlin is amazed by the poses, by the props, by the cruel timing of the scene before her. But its content and its meaning both carry the crushing weight of the inevitable. And as five years' worth of suspicions are confirmed, Caitlin Chaisson learns that she is not the plucky, courageous woman she has seen in movies. Because though it pains her beyond measure, she can't even bring herself to move, much less throw the bathroom door open and drag her husband out into the hallway by his hair. Indeed, her right foot is still hovering in the air just behind her; she's yet to complete the final step that brought her here.

And so Caitlin Chaisson begins backing down the stairs, and by the time she turns around, she finds the foyer empty—the last of the party's attendees are but shadows outside as they follow the flickering ghostly halo of Willie's lantern down the oak-lined gravel path that leads to the guest parking lot by the levee.

Through the double parlor she runs past the giant painting of the grand Greek Revival house as it looked before its destruction in 1850, past the caterers who are cleaning up in the kitchen; they do their job to perfection, never noticing the woman of the house as she sprints past them, her breaths turning to shallow coughs.

It is on the railing of the back porch that she sees it: half-empty, lipstick-smudged. After any other party it would have been an irritant when she passed it the next morning, but tonight it is the instrument of her salvation. She picks up the champagne flute, smashes it against the porch rail, and continues to run.

5

2

By the time Caitlin reaches the gazebo, she has tried several times to begin the incision, and the results are a series of claw marks on her left arm that are oozing a thin layer of blood. The floorboards give her footfalls greater resonance than the muddy paths she traveled through manicured gardens to get here, and this sharp, staccato reminder that she is still among the living forces her to reconsider her decision. Now she finds herself spinning in place, the shattered rim of the champagne flute dripping blood onto the gazebo's floor.

The overhead light inside the gazebo is off. The great house is a vision of antebellum perfection beyond what was once the plantation's sprawling cane field, but is now a maze of brick planters, flagstone walkways, and small fountains—the latter of which make an insistent, nagging gurgle in the absence of laughter and party chatter.

This moment of quiet is all she needs for years' worth of warnings and admonishments to fill the silence, a riot in her head that shoves out all reasonable and adult voices, that has her spinning in place, her grip on the broken champagne flute growing tighter even as she tries to relax her hand.

No shadows have pursued her. No guilty husband is striding toward her across the watery lawns.

Why should he? No wound in her soul could ever be deep enough to draw his mouth from that whore's pale, young flesh. Perhaps if she had screamed . . . But she is alone now with the terrible knowledge that, in her husband's eyes, she really is just freckled Caitlin with the down-turned mouth that gives her a constant frown and the pinprick eyes that too closely crowd the bridge of her nose, the girl with the sloping shoulders and the skinny neck that's always been too long for her frame, the awkward one, the one everyone looks over in an attempt to get a better view of the *real* prizes that carry the Chaisson family name: the mansion on St. Charles Avenue, the postcard-perfect plantation, and the libraries and museums named for her grandfather.

Back in high school, Caitlin overheard a teacher—not some bitchy fellow student, but an actual *teacher*—say of her, "The Chaissons may be loaded, but all the money in the world isn't going to drag that girl over from the ugly side of plain." And now it's clear her husband is no different from that vile, hateful woman, despite the fact that he gave all the right answers during the neurotic, late-night interrogations she's subjected him to over the years.

And yet there *were* warnings. Years of them, mostly subtle. When her mother was still alive, for example, the struggle not to speak up had practically torn the woman apart, and somehow, witnessing that restrained torment out of the corner of her eye had been worse for Caitlin than some outright confrontation over whether or not her handsome, charming husband really loved her.

And then there was Blake, her closest friend in the world . . . until he'd actually come to her with evidence. He had friends who worked at the casinos in Biloxi, and they'd seen Troy there with other women, even after Troy had promised never to gamble away another dime of their money (her money, her money, *her* money!)

again. It was almost enough to dismiss the fact that he'd done so while in the company of various sluts (and even now she couldn't help wonder if one of them had been the whore getting *fingered-fuckedsuckedlicked* by her husband right now . . .).

And what had she done?

First she accused Blake of being ungrateful. *After everything Troy did for you when he was a cop!* Then, when that tactic didn't shame Blake into silence, she accused Blake of having romantic feelings for Troy, of getting all tangled up in their long, complex history. After all, years before he married Caitlin, Troy was Blake's savior, the man who had brought him swift and lasting justice. Perhaps, since then, Blake had decided he wanted Troy to be his knight in shining armor in every possible way! Hell, maybe he'd been nursing feelings for Troy ever since they'd all first met. It had been bullshit, of course. Utter and complete bullshit, but she'd hurled it right at his face rather than accept the horrible truth Blake had delivered with a bowed head and averted eyes.

In the six months since they last spoke, it has been impossible not to see the stunned and wounded look on Blake Henderson's face every time she closes her eyes and tries to sleep.

The rock walls in her mind that keep a life's worth of painful memories from meeting in a single river of fiery self-hate have collapsed entirely. Her present humiliation flows right through the doors of that long-ago hospital room where Blake made a confession far more devastating than the one he'd made six months ago about Troy's gambling. He'd been recovering from a brutal assault at the time, medicated out of his head for the pain. And it was her fault, really. She was the one who'd made the mistake of going back in, of asking him later if the tale he'd told her about her father was something more than a morphine-fueled delusion. Drug-fueled perhaps, Blake had admitted, but not a delusion.

When they were just freshmen in high school, her father offered Blake money to have a romantic relationship with her. Not just money, but scaled incentives that would increase over time, all to remain in an intimate, sexual relationship with his teenage daughter. First a nice car when Blake was old enough to drive, then money for a decent college when the time came, and after that, if he actually saw fit to marry her, who knew? A house? A career? Blake had turned him down, of course, mostly with nodding and stunned silence. But the story wasn't about Blake, or what he did or didn't do. The story was about a father so convinced his daughter was irredeemably ugly he felt he had no choice but to arrange her marriage to a fourteen-year-old boy who was clearly on the road to homosexuality. What was it that had convinced her father she was so unattractive, so profoundly unlovable? Was it her stork-like neck? Her impossible, wiry hair?

They had all seen, all of them. Blake. Her mother. Her father. They'd seen the lie at the heart of her marriage and tried to warn her in their own pained and desperate ways. Now they were gone, all of them—her parents incinerated in a single instant when their Cessna crashed to the earth, and Blake driven away by her vengeful misuse of one of the most painful episodes of his life.

Alone—not a hazy, vague feeling that's sure to pass in time. A diagnosis. A terminal condition. Just her and the continuous, eye-watering vision of her husband driving his hand between the thighs of that pretty little blonde, who had been smiling graciously at Caitlin across a room full of her friends just an hour before. Had the girl also stared smugly at her through the crack in the bathroom door even as Caitlin's husband lifted her up onto the vanity? Or was she imagining that now?

A few months after they were married, Troy used a demonstration of the right pose and angle for a real suicide cut as a prelude to more pleasurable matters, standing behind her as he gently dragged

a fork up the length of her wrist. "This is how you do it if you're serious about something other than getting attention from the other
kids," he'd explained. And after she'd taken over, he'd whispered
in her ear, "Good form, baby," before he slid one hand around the
back of her thigh and clamped the other over her chest so he could
hold her in place when she started to writhe under the sudden,
fierce ministrations of his fingers. At the time it had all seemed
dangerous and sexy. How else would a cop do foreplay? But had
there been more violence in the display than she'd been willing to
see? Had he just been tutoring her for a moment like this one? Had
he been imagining her eventual suicide with a murderer's intent?

Caitlin presses the jagged lip of the shattered champagne flute
against her wrist until she sees the flesh give from the pressure; then
she drags it slowly up the length of her forearm. The wound flows,
but isn't the sloppy, arterial burst she was aiming for. Even so, a tremendous heat travels up the length of her arm, so intense she doesn't
realize she's dropped her makeshift dagger until she hears it hit the
floor. But the heat is more pressure than pure flame, and it is a relief
compared to the Indian burn she felt inside her gut when Troy's teeth
fastened around that pretty young woman's earlobe. It feels as if her
left arm is turning to vapor, and she's half convinced the crackling
sound she hears is her own blood hitting the gazebo's floor.

But the soft series of pops that come next has to be cracking
wood. That can mean only one thing and it's absurd: something is
chewing the gazebo itself.

Impossible . . .

Caitlin clamps her hand over the flowing wound. Her suicidal
conviction has evaporated at the first signs of either a monster or
a miracle, she isn't sure. The dark tendrils curling up through the
fresh cracks in the gazebo's floor have started a serpentine crawl
toward the splatter of blood at her feet.

They are snakes gone boneless, she thinks. That's how they've squeezed through the cracks in the gazebo's floor. But when they continue to rise straight up into the air with strength and determination, when their fat, wrist-thick bodies don't droop or bend, when she sees not one, not two, but four tendrils in all, rising on all sides of her in an almost perfect circle, she glances down at her hand, at the tiny rivers of blood spilling in between her fingers, to see if her blood loss is severe enough to cause hallucinations. But while the pain is still there, the flow is too slight, hitting the jostled floorboards in fat intermittent drops. She isn't near death, that's for sure. And the shock of almost walking in on her husband fucking another woman has pushed the champagne rapidly through her system, leaving her stone-cold sober and alert.

Caitlin can see clearly alternating patches of strange luminescence lining the slender bodies of these strange creatures. And while everything about their size and their behavior is utterly wrong, their composition is simple, common even.

"Flowers and leaves . . ."

She whispers these words to herself.

Not snakes, not the fingers of some subterranean beast. Vines. That's all. But once she's whispered these words aloud—*flowers and leaves*—the words only deepen her paralysis, because by then she can see that the blossoms, each one about the size of her hand, are opening in unison. They look like the flowers of a calla lily, but inside of their four, evenly sized white petals is an insect-like amalgam of stamens and filaments, and all of it glows with an interior radiance so powerful it looks like it might drift away, spirit-like, from the temporary prison of the petals.

And each blossom, each impossibly animated, pulsing blossom, is pointed directly at her.

They're looking at me.

Then the smell hits her, a force as powerful and determined as the vines themselves, plugging her nostrils, making her eyes water. She hears her own quick, deep breaths as if from a distance, a ragged counterpoint to the sounds of the floorboards underfoot settling back into their new disturbed positions. The smell is blanketing her, consuming her. She blinks madly, trying to resist its call, because not only is it somehow drawing in darkness from the edges of her vision, but it is also nothing like the cloying perfumes she has always associated with Spring House.

It is the smell of fire.

. . . They are coming.

She can feel the horse hooves pounding the mud, can feel them through the channel she has opened in the palms of her callused hands, the ones that connect her to the clamor of angry souls within the soil. She can hear their shouts. They have discovered the decimated cane field, and they know what she has done. That after promising them a limitless bounty, she has punished them for their betrayal.

And because they have some sense of what she is capable of, they will come with their polished Colt revolvers, and they will attack with as much swiftness as they can muster. And so she has no time to wait. She must bring herself to the very raw edge of her power, the place where she can feel a writhing, feral chaos in the darkness on the other side.

The darkness below. The darkness underfoot.

She's always pulled back from that place, not in fear that she wouldn't be able to stop the result, but in fear that it would tear her apart from within. But now the choice is to either die by their lead, or summon forth a final justice from an earth that has always spoken to her in a magical language only she seems to hear.

Because they are angry. They are seeking their own twisted form of justice, and this fact leaves her with the despairing realization that all forms of justice are somehow twisted at their core. Will Felix Delachaise be among them, or will he leave the bloodiest work to his overseer as usual, the same overseer whose work she halted in mid-whip, beginning this whole mess?

But when the door to the slave quarters behind her blows open, she sees neither the overseer nor Spring House's bastard owner. She sees a perfectly framed view of her husband, Troy Mangier, halfway out of his suit, bare ass flexing as he drives himself into the beautiful young woman. And Caitlin feels herself jostled inside of her dreaming point of view—who was it? A slave?

The past and present have met in a fever dream of rage, and now her husband is staring slack-jawed at her through a doorway—in time, in history, in sanity, she can't know—while he continues to fuck some little slut atop the bathroom sink. But the rage is leaving her. Maybe because Troy is staring at her over one shoulder, mouth open, eyes vacant. His expression is devoid of lust; his thrusts seem compulsory now. The floor between them explodes, and with the exhalation of her crippling rage, Caitlin senses the arrival of a strange new power.

3

"Not here," Troy whispers.

And that's when Jane Percival realizes why he won't take his hand out from his Hanes, even though she's pushed back over the porcelain sink so far the copper faucet is digging into her spine, even though her dress is hiked so far up her legs he's been able to work wonders on her with his mouth for a good five minutes now—his blood isn't pumping to all the right places yet, and he doesn't want to let on.

What does he want? A short walk, a little caffeine? Neither will be easy to come by with the wife hovering somewhere downstairs.

Is she hovering, Jane wonders, *or is she passed out drunk somewhere?*

Caitlin Chaisson spent most of the night glaring at Jane like she was some party crasher, and all night long Jane fought the urge to get right up in the girl's face and let her know that while he was singing "Happy Birthday" with the rest of them, Caitlin's husband was winking at Jane across the room and dragging his top teeth across his bottom lip like he could taste her on it.

Happy Birthday, princess!

Still, she hadn't planned to move quite this fast, because she hadn't been prepared for how epically drunk her target was going to be. Just the thought of having to stop now sends a spike of panic through Jane. Her first choice would have been slow seduction, not a frenzied quickie in the upstairs bathroom. But in her experience nothing killed a long game faster than a false start, or a suddenly remorseful husband buttoning up his pants and racing for the confessional booth. And tonight had taken weeks of subtle but careful preparation, weeks of listening studiously as her best friend, Margot, gossiped about the loveless marriage between her two wealthiest clients, one a former hero cop her aunt Judy would have described as *crap your pants handsome*, the other a spoiled-rotten trust-fund baby who went through life looking like she'd just smelled something terrible and it was you.

It wasn't an easy sell, getting Margot to take her on as a crew supervisor for bigger events, events like Skanky Chaisson's birthday party. The two women met when Jane worked the bar for one of Margot's first events after she started Simply Splendid eight years ago. Since then, Jane had pitched in at all levels of the business, except for supervisor. Still, Jane wasn't interested in passing trays; she was pretty damn sure the unflattering black-and-white uniform would make it that much harder to catch Troy Mangier's eye. Instead she'd pitched Margot hard on the position that would allow her to wear a sparkly, low-cut cocktail dress, enabling her to look as classy and elegant as most of the other invited guests.

But now Jane is missing in action during teardown, her target is on the edge of bailing, and there's a possibly suspicious wife somewhere nearby.

Good Christ, if Margot gets wind of even half of this, Jane will be in a world of trouble far bigger than an angry wife pounding on the door with the side of one fist.

Troy Mangier pulls up his trousers by his belt buckle and takes a step back, forcing Jane to unwrap her legs from around his waist. The way she sees it, she's only got two options: try for the

15

remorseful, romance-novel routine of *I'm so sorry I forced myself on you*—even though she hadn't, technically—*but my feelings for you are just sooooooo strong*, or drop to her knees and take him in her mouth right there.

But before she can commit to either, Troy Mangier takes her by the hand and pulls her off the sink. Her feet land gracelessly on top of her high heels instead of sliding into them cleanly, and Troy grabs her by the waist to make sure she doesn't lose her balance as the shoes crumple under her feet like foliage.

Their lips meet in a sloppy kiss that fills her mouth with scotch breath, and Troy Mangier says, "Come with me."

4

The hallucination breaks, giving way to a reality inside the gazebo that is more dreamlike and impossible than any of the visions that just strobed across her mind's eye.

At the moment when Caitlin is sure her knees are going to strike the gazebo's floor, a slick tendril wraps around her throat and she cries out, sure she's about to be choked. But it does nothing of the kind. Rather, with a gentleness that seems almost human, it rights her until she is standing on both feet once again, before it slips off her shoulder, slides briefly down her left breast, and hovers in the air in front of her, level with her chest. In the pulses of light that line the stalks of each vine, she sees a clover-like assembly of leaves unfurling at its tip, opening to her just as the blossoms have. Only nothing glows within these leaves. They contain darkness deeper than the vague, shadowy definitions inside the gazebo.

But there is no misinterpreting the gesture; it's as delicate and unnervingly polite as the sudden catch that kept her from falling knees-first to the floor.

She can vividly recall each vision that came from the scent of the blossoms, the jostled, terrifying flashbacks and the absolute certainty she was inside the body of some long-dead slave, the sense of imminent attack—*they are coming!*—but then, at the very end, her own husband, followed by the miraculous sense of the rage draining from her.

Draining, the word occurs to her easily, instinctively, and she remembers the eagerness with which the first tendrils that poked up through the floor pursued her fresh drops of blood. And that's when she realizes what the unfurled leaves and the helpful vine hovering in the air before her look like—an extended hand.

A soft pop comes from the direction of the main house, the sound of someone trying—too late—to keep a screen door from slamming behind them. Peering between the vines, Caitlin sees them: Troy and the little slut.

Two silhouettes moving down the back of the house, crouching down to avoid the kitchen windows before they hurry through the maze of fountains and flower planters, bound for the oak-shadowed corridor on the opposite side of the property that houses the gardening shed. They are oblivious to her, where she stands shrouded by magic and shadow.

The girl almost trips, which causes her to throw her hand to her mouth to stifle her startled cry, and Troy curves an arm around her shoulders, and together, they stumble toward the shed.

As she watches her husband and his little slut join the darkness, Caitlin craves that cleansing feeling that marked the very end of the violent vision quest the blossoms just gave her—that sense that the rage she feels toward Troy has been expelled from her like a breath she's held in for half a minute too long. Even if it means being rocketed back inside the body of that terrified slave. Even if it means unleashing some greater power from the inexplicable monster before her.

Caitlin extends her bleeding wrist toward the hovering vine. A thirsty pulse moves through the blossoms as it wraps firmly around her open wound. No visions come to her, but the sensation that accompanies the vine's patient suckling is like a dozen sets of hands gently dragging their fingernails across her skin from her scalp to her toes. Her cry has more abandon in it than any sound she heard Troy's little whore make in the guest bathroom.

As the vine slides down her wrist, then slips gently free of her palm and fingers, she sees that she has been healed; all that remains of her determined gash is a pale, rosy scar. Before she has time to process the implication of this, the thick tendrils on all sides of her descend cleanly through the spaces between the floorboards.

Barely a minute later, the earth shifts violently underneath one of the fountains in the center of the garden. The impact from below jostles the fountain's copper basin to such an angle that the water begins pouring out of it in a thin and steady stream. A few seconds later, a tiny stone cherub is knocked from its perch, and several bricks along the side of a flower planter have been knocked free. Caitlin realizes they are but pieces of a contrail from some healing force that is now moving through the soil in pursuit of her husband's sin.

5

Jane is amazed by the power of desire.

She is terrified of dark places, especially this far out in the country, and on any other night this pitch-black gardening shed would be an un-enterable lair of coiled snakes and patient psychopaths. But tonight, with Troy Mangier palming her and suckling her and taking her in a lust-stuttered waltz across the dirt floor, the darkness liberates.

Jane has watched every single one of his TV appearances she can find on YouTube, dating back to when he first solved the John Fuller murder. She recalls the same features that are currently concealed by shadows, the sight of Troy's swoon-worthy jawline and thick, muscular neck. These fragmented memories juxtapose with the reality of his fingers working their way inside of her and intensify the delicious, toe-curling thrill of ambition meeting lust. So when she hears a strange crackling sound, she assumes it's her own dress being torn away from her.

When Troy goes still, Jane takes this as her cue. She reaches for his crotch and is relieved when her hand closes around something hard and thick. She starts to stroke him—it's much bigger than she expected—and she's trying to think of the nastiest, dirtiest way to say this to him when she realizes something about the thing isn't right. The surface of his cock is spiny and slick.

When she realizes the darkness has tricked her, Jane stumbles backward. She sees Troy's shadow bent at the waist; the fluid-filled, throaty sounds coming from him are not strangled, lustful groans. *Choking. He's choking.* A thick strand of shadow juts from his open mouth and up toward the dark ceiling; a sliver of light from the nearby window falls across its spiny length.

The thing Jane just released from her right hand has the body and tense energy of a serpent, and it has now reached an elephantine length in the darkness between her and Troy, curving at the tip, coated in a slick substance that has to be blood. *Troy's blood . . . because the damn thing has punched right through his—they're connected. Holy shit. It's the same goddamn thing and it's gone RIGHT THROUGH—*

Jane falls ass-first to the floor before this deranged thought can complete itself. The first scream will feel too much like a surrender, so she tries to screw her jaw shut, which even then has her cursing madly under her breath as she scrambles toward the wall and its racks of gardening tools.

By the time she's closed her hands around the handle of the axe hanging on a nearby shelf, two more snakes of darkness have punched up through the dirty floor, and Jane Percival glimpses the impossible luminescence coursing through one shimmering white blossom before its petals open like a snake's jaws . . . and the entire flower clamps down over Troy Mangier's bulging right eye.

A white pulse streaks through the flower, then the pulse becomes a bright-green glow that courses through the entire tangle of stalks, illuminating its growing, snarled structure. The flower and Troy's flesh have merged somehow, and the vine just behind the flower swells in thickness. And then Troy's head has vanished inside a thickening tangle of . . . she's about to think of them as snakes

21

again, but even as she pulls the axe free from its shelf, a very steady voice inside of her head corrects her: *Vines. They are vines. Look . . .*

And because she can't bring herself to scream just yet, because only decisive action will hold the nightmarish impossibility of all of this at bay, Jane Percival draws the axe back over one shoulder and swings. She is convinced that one good whack will send this creature back down into the ground, that a thing without eyes and a face will react to any swift and terrible blow with pure fear and total retreat.

And yet it doesn't, and she's distracted by the sound she made when the axe hit its shifting, growing target—a raspy grunt that threatens sobs. Then she understands. She feels the hot, wet spray and sees how terrible her aim was. The blade has sliced clean through a knot of vine around Troy's leg, and the eruption of blood is fearsome, arterial, and the vines do not retreat. Rather, they close thirstily over the wound instead, and suddenly Troy Mangier is completely entombed.

The vines are crawling up and over the spot where his head and shoulders were just an instant before, and now they're coming down on themselves, making a shape that tells her Troy has been devoured from the crown of his head to the center of his chest. She realizes the rest of him is almost gone too, and that's when Jane Percival finally starts to scream.

6

When the screaming starts, Nova Thomas is washing Caitlin Chaisson's best china and wondering whether or not to tell her father she saw Troy sneak off into the garden with one of the pretty white ladies from the catering company. Troy must have been drunk as a skunk—otherwise he would have known to pull off his shiny gold necktie. But he didn't, and the thing winked at Nova each time the shadowy couple passed just outside the halo of one of the security lights fixed on the back of the house.

For the past few minutes since he escorted the last guests to their parked cars, Nova's father has been proudly telling stories about Spring House like he, Willie Thomas, owned the place, all the while pouring leftover champagne for the catering staff and valets, who are cleaning the kitchen in a controlled frenzy. But Nova's glass of bubbly sits sparkling and untouched on the counter beside her. It feels strangely like a bribe from the birthday girl herself, and after three years at LSU listening to professors lecture on the real and bloody history of sugarcane plantations like Spring House, Nova isn't all that inclined to celebrate some spoiled white lady who lives off her dead parents and still treats Nova as if she were a dumb child.

Then a woman is screaming somewhere out in the dark, and Nova's resentments are forgotten. Her father stands frozen, an upended champagne bottle in hand.

When the overflows, the chef reaches up and rights the bottle, but he too is staring out the large picture window toward the shadowy gardens and the source of those terrible, piercing screams.

The bottle smashes to the floor as Willie runs out the back door. Nova runs after him.

She's one hundred percent sure Caitlin's found her husband with that girl in the shed, and now all hell's about to break loose. And what if Troy's got some kind of gun or who knows what? And the way her daddy is with Caitlin (*Miss* Caitlin to him, every time), always acting like her happy house Negro, he's bound to do something stupid to defend her and—

"Daddy, stop. *Daddy!*"

Her foot catches on something. Her hands break her fall on the flagstone path. When she looks back, she sees that some kind of eruption in the planter behind her has tossed several bricks onto her path.

By the time he throws open the door to the gardening shed, Nova is struggling to her feet, scanning her surroundings, trying to get her balance.

What happens next has the quality of a dream's last few minutes, that moment just before the dreamer starts to awake—crystal clear but somehow paper-thin and unreal.

The woman who explodes from the shed is so covered in dirt and blood Nova doesn't recognize her. What she does recognize, though, is that she's got an axe raised over one shoulder, and when she swings it, Nova lets out a sound that is more animal than human. The earth seems to fly by under her feet, but it's not enough—the head of the axe is aimed straight at her father, and her breath freezes in her lungs as she leaps.

He ducks. The blade nicks his shoulder anyway, and he goes down. Nova leaps before the woman has time to raise the axe again. There's no fight in the woman's body when Nova slams her against the wall of the shed. Nova realizes the woman has dropped the axe only when both of the lunatic's dirt-smeared hands are fending off Nova's blows.

"You crazy bitch!" Nova hears herself scream. "You crazy white bitch!"

Her father is shouting her name with a strength and confidence that tells her he's not badly injured. But her anger is a wild and uncontrollable thing; it flows copiously through valves that have been opened in her only recently by education and history and a new sense of self that one of her professors defined as *personhood*.

Some stupid white girl's not going to chop my daddy down like he's a damn tree. I don't think so! No ma'am.

At first Nova thinks it's her father who has pulled her off the crazed woman—who has sunk to a crouch and is sobbing hysterically, hands raised to defend herself. But the voice in Nova's ear is soft, and almost a whisper. It's Caitlin.

"Oh gosh," Caitlin says, sounding more dazed than panicked. "Now what on earth is happening *here*?"

Gosh? Nova thinks. *Caitlin's as crazy as this bitch covered in blood.*

The woman collapsed in front of the shed has lost her mind, it seems. Her legs splayed, she's pumping her hands in front of her face like she's trying to disperse a cloud of invisible insects.

Caitlin steps over the crazy woman and into the darkness beyond. Despite her lingering anger, Nova is astonished by the woman's bravery, by the way she pushes the door open just enough to allow herself to step inside what is surely a scene of bloody horror.

"Miss Caitlin," Willie calls out to her, and Caitlin turns, one finger raised to quiet him. The nod she gives them is both calm and authoritative, as if she is relieving them of their solemn duty so she can face whatever bloody nightmare must be inside the shed alone.

And that's when Nova sees it. It is small and it is glowing, and it appears to be hovering just above the shed's dirt floor. Her first guess is that it's one of those glow-in-the-dark sticks that come with the emergency kits she buys her father for hurricane season, the kind you crack in both hands to illuminate. But there are too many different bright colors pulsating in it—and she can't think of why one of those would be in the shed in the first place.

Nova is riveted by the sight of the . . . *flower? Is it some kind of flower? Maybe some decoration stolen from inside the—*

Caitlin is looking back at her.

It's easy to miss in the shadows, but the woman is most certainly staring back over one shoulder at Nova, and there is nothing startled or solicitous about her expression. She needs no confirmation from Nova that she too has witnessed the strange, shimmering apparition. Instead, she reaches back and shuts the door behind her, leaving Nova with the conviction that Caitlin knows exactly what the damn thing is and doesn't want anyone else to see it.

7

We are not that family, Nova thinks, once the police have separated her from her father.

He is outside now with the uniformed officers who arrived within minutes of the first 911 call, while the two plainclothes detectives who appear to be leading the investigation into Troy's disappearance have brought Nova to the house's grand front parlor.

God only knows where Caitlin is. Probably upstairs, laid out on one of the canopied beds, the cops tending to her like nursemaids, even though it's very possible she's the one who started this entire mess. But Nova can't go there just yet; she's still not sure what the hell that thing was inside of the shed, right where Troy Mangier should have been lying in a bloody tumble of limbs. And so she's still not sure what, if anything, Caitlin is hiding from them all.

The hardwood floor under their feet is dappled with glitter and confetti. Caitlin's presents, brought by those who insisted on ignoring the invitation's polite promise *Your presence is our gift,* sit in a shiny pile atop a side table sandwiched between two of the house's soaring front windows and their lush, puddling drapes. And even though she is trying to look submissive and polite—*respectful,* as her mother would have said, usually after bopping Nova across the behind with a rolled-up magazine because she said something smart—a defensive monologue is building in Nova's throat like steam inside of a calliope.

We were not the family the cops came to. We were not the family with some son or brother or uncle who'd given himself over to the law of the street and came banging on our doors and waving guns at all hours of the night. My daddy is alive. He works too damn hard and my mother died of cancer, and goddammit, I have never touched a gun in my life, and I shouldn't be here being questioned by these two smug cops as if I've got something to do with the insanity of some crazy blood-covered white lady.

This is the first time Nova has been invited to sit on any of the antique furniture, and only because the two cops suggested she take a seat, probably so they could tower over her like they're doing now. The bald one studies her closely, while the one with the hairpiece leads the charge, each question tinged with something that sounds more like amusement than suspicion. They smell of too much Old Spice, which suggests they knew which house they were visiting, knew the type of fancy folks they'd be talking to.

Except for her, of course. She is the daughter of the help. If she comes off as sounding too educated, she'll be the uppity bitch with something to hide. If she plays it cool and quiet, they'll dismiss her as ignorant and weak. (And if she says anything about strangely glowing flowers, they'll laugh her off as some wannabe voodoo queen.)

Gripping one hand in the other does nothing to quiet her nerves, or her anger, so she tells herself this is how cops talk to everyone—dismissive, holier-than-thou. Maybe the TV shows have it right, or maybe the cops have started to watch too many TV shows. But that's got to be it. They're not talking to her like this because she's black, and they're not treating her this way just to punish her for being a young black woman who speaks with greater

28

eloquence than they do. *They're not. They're not. They're not,* she tries to assure herself.

"I said she worked for the catering company," Nova answers for the third time.

"Still," Hairpiece asks. "You'd never seen her before. Company's been working parties here for a few years now, we heard, but this girl's new?"

"Have you asked her?" Nova counters.

"We're letting her calm down first."

"Good luck. She doesn't seem very calm to me."

"But tonight's the first night you met?"

"We didn't meet, officially. She was supervising . . . sort of. But I saw her at the start of the party and not much after. Until I saw them running toward the shed."

"How'd you know it was them?"

"Troy's necktie. It was shiny, gold. He could have landed planes with it. Fool should have known to take it off if he was going to . . ."

"Going to what?"

"Well, I don't think they we're going out there to get a shovel."

"But Miss Percival—you've never seen her before tonight?"

"No, I've never seen her before, but I don't work every party . . ." *Because Daddy knows if he makes me work every one without pay, I might haul off and give Caitlin the whack she deserves.* She is not like her daddy's neighbors; she is not the type of black person who believes that seven hours of work—three hours of smiling at white folks, and then two hours of manual labor on either side of that—should be compensated with a trunk full of leftover liquor. For one, she's never had a real taste for the hard stuff. Second, she's a bigger fan of fair wages and progress than she is of cases of Diet Coke and a pat on the head.

"So she's still not talking?" Nova asks.

"Let's not focus on her."

"She almost killed my father. You think we should be focused on something else?"

"Story we heard is you did a fine job of coming to your daddy's defense."

"Thank you."

"Like maybe you were ready . . ."

"Ready? For *what*?"

"Whole thing went down pretty fast is what I'm saying. Girl starts screaming, your father starts running like he recognizes the sound."

"Screaming is hard to recognize?" Nova asks.

"Like he recognized who was doing the screaming."

"What'd y'all find inside that shed?" she asks.

"What do you think we should have found?"

A flower, she thinks. *A glowing flower that didn't make any damn sense, something so crazy and surreal you wouldn't be bothering me with this crap about Daddy if you'd seen it, and if you haven't seen it, that means Caitlin's hiding it.*

Focus, she tells herself. *Focus on where they're trying to lead you and keep it from going there.*

How many parties did that dumb skank work? Why were you so prepared to keep her from whacking his head off? How *involved* was your big black daddy with the pretty young white girl who for some reason tried to butcher him?

"Look, I saw Troy Mangier headed out to the shed with that girl—"

"But you didn't see Troy come out?"

"Because he *didn't* come out."

"You didn't *see* him—"

"I didn't see him come out because he didn't come out. There's no back door, so unless he managed to dig his way out in about five minutes' time, then I don't know where you think he's going to be."

For the first time, her words have unsettled the two white men standing over her, and she's willing to bet it's the phrase *dig his way out* that caused Baldy to shoot his partner a nervous, fleeting glance.

"You still live with your daddy?" Baldy asks quietly. There's a hurried tone to the question, as if he's eager to get them back on script. And she hates the familiar way he's referred to her father. Sure, she calls him Daddy in everyday conversation still. Most children of the South, white or black, do the same with their own fathers. But Willie is not this man's father. (He's not Caitlin's damn daddy either, but watching them together most days, you would think so.)

"Not full time, no," she answers.

"Where do you live?" Hairpiece asks.

"I'm at LSU. I told you."

"Still, where do you live?"

"A dorm. Where do you—" She stops herself before she makes a joke about separate dorms for whites and coloreds. But the startled expression on the detective's face makes the point for her. The ensuing moment is so awkward the two detectives can't look her in the eye. It's doubtful Hairpiece actually thought the dorms were segregated. But Nova figures these country detectives are so unaccustomed to dealing with black college students, they simply assumed all the terms would be different. Or they assumed that black people don't use the word *dorm*.

For several years now, Nova Thomas has longed to join her father, Caitlin, and so many of the other people around her in their cozy dreams about the past. If only, like so many of the white people she goes to school with, she could look at the history of places like Spring House and see only singing, dancing African slaves freed from the burden of owning property and patiently awaiting the divine justice of President Abraham Lincoln. But college is deepening her long-held suspicion that she grew up being told less than

31

one-quarter of the real story about Spring House, the real story of Louisiana itself, and she can't help but wonder if all of this—this interrogation, not to mention washing dishes in Spring House's kitchen on a regular basis—would be easier if she hadn't sat down with Dr. Taylor during office hours a few months ago and helped her figure out the exact spot on the property where the sons of Felix Delachaise used to line up to rape the new female slaves.

One thing is for sure. She's not telling these cops about that damn flower. She will, however, check out that shed as soon as they're gone so she can find out why the idea of Troy digging his way out made Baldy look at Hairpiece like he'd farted. But if she's going to risk angering the cops in one way, she might as well allow herself another. *All right, voodoo queen's out,* she thinks. *Time for uppity Negro.*

"My father doesn't have sex with white ladies," Nova says quietly. "Ever. Don't get me wrong. There's been a lot of women since my mother died, and I wasn't a fan of most of them. But none of them were white, and none of them carried an axe, and none of them were low-account trash that would go out to the shed with another woman's husband at that woman's birthday party. So how about y'all quit this scenario where my father's bending over backward into crazy because some white lady might have paid him some attention? Then maybe you'll find out where Troy Mangier *really* is."

Her heart races. She can already feel the handcuffs closing around her wrists. But the sensation is fantasy and nothing more because, just then, Baldy turns and walks out of the room and Hairpiece thanks her for her time, and suddenly Nova is all by herself in the front parlor of Spring House for the first time, her hands still trembling even as she clasps them between her knees.

8

Blake Henderson is just a few paces from the automatic doors to the emergency room when he sees the father of the first man to die in his arms.

Vernon Fuller drives the same 1988 Chevy Suburban he did when Blake was a boy, with its boxy nose and fat navy-blue side stripe. The first weak light of an overcast dawn dapples the windshield with the reflections of oak branches, turning Vernon into a vague, baseball-capped silhouette behind the wheel. As usual, the SUV is parked in one of the metered spaces on Prytania Street just across from the entrance to Touro Infirmary.

It's been a long night—five gunshots, one overdose, and two violent psych cases. The kind of night that would cause a normal person to grimace when they heard the list of admissions rattled off in sequence, but which leaves adrenaline-addicted nurses like Blake amped and incapable of sleep, even after fourteen hours on the floor.

So even though he's fairly sure how this will go, Blake starts across Prytania Street, devoid of traffic at this early hour, and toward the Suburban. For a few seconds, the only sounds he hears are his tennis shoes slapping the pavement and his scrubs scraping against his legs. Then the Suburban's engine starts up, and its headlights wink on, and it swerves to avoid Blake at the last second before speeding off in the direction of the Garden District.

If history is any indicator, Blake will spend the next few nights waiting for a late-night hang-up. Or an e-mail from an unfamiliar address. Any indication that Vernon Fuller wants something more than a predawn glimpse. Then Blake will forget about Vernon Fuller altogether until the next slightly menacing and unexplained visit. Vernon's son, on the other hand, will live on forever in Blake's memories and nightmares.

Especially the feel of his bound wrists as Blake tried desperately to free him before the black water rose to swallow them both.

When the phone rings and an unfamiliar number flashes on the screen, Blake is sure it's Vernon, breaking their fifteen-year silence. He's not sure what to feel: dread or relief? Will it be a good thing? The old man has never allowed the only other man who loved his son as much as he did to join him in his grief, and maybe there's a reason for that. A good reason. But when he hits "Accept," the voice on the other end isn't his dead lover's father, but something quaky and female.

"Something's wrong out here," Nova Thomas says.

"Is your dad OK?"

"He's gonna be . . . Listen, I know y'all had a fight and all, but . . ."

"But what?"

"You need to talk to Caitlin."

"About what?" he asks, suddenly wary.

"There was a party here last night . . ." He fights the urge to tell her he knows full well Caitlin's birthday party is always held on the Saturday closest to her actual birthday, that he picked up a double shift last night to distract himself from the pain of not attending for the first time since they were kids. "And Troy . . ."

They aren't the best of friends, but Blake knows Nova Thomas well enough to know that she is strong-willed and intelligent and not prone to this kind of stammering and disjointed thinking. "Troy went into the gardening shed with some woman from the catering company"—Blake feels a surge of triumph at this terrible news, and then a wave of guilt—"but he didn't come out. Just the girl did. And she was bloody and had an axe—"

That's when Blake sees the two men walking casually toward the automatic doors he just stepped through moments before. About the same height, one sporting a hairpiece, the other balding with pride. Their plain, mid-priced dress shirts are tucked so tightly into their khakis he wonders if they've laced the shirttails through the insides of their briefs. All the telltale signs are there, but it's the forced-casual gait combined with the slow and steady pivoting of their necks that tells Blake who they are. There was a time in his life when he became intimately familiar with the look of homicide detectives, and he fears that another one is about to begin.

"Are the police involved?"

"*Involved?* You mean, like . . . with the axe?"

"No, I mean, did you talk to them."

"Yeah. Baldy and Hairpiece. They were a real treat."

"They're about to be mine."

"All right, well. Feel free to use my nicknames."

"Is he dead, Nova?" Blake asks. Just then, he sees one of the cops turn. He's spotted Blake's reflection in the automatic doors. "Troy, I mean. Did Caitlin . . ."

"I don't know," Nova answers. "I don't know what she did or what she didn't do. But there's something . . . He just . . ."

"Gone . . . ," Blake says, distracted by the two detectives who are now walking straight toward him, plastic half smiles on their deeply lined faces.

"Just please . . . come see me when you can. There's something else I gotta talk to you about."

"I'll call you back," he says to her, but she has already hung up on him, and the first detective has already mounted the curb and is extending his hand in greeting.

9

The detectives suggest Coulis, a little restaurant a block from the hospital that looks like a hole-in-the-wall but hosts long lines of customers every weekend who are willing to wait outside patiently for a plate of eggs Benedict with roast beef debris. And Blake knows it is well worth it. He also knows, though, that the place won't be open for half an hour, so they settle on the drab hospital cafeteria.

"I haven't seen or spoken to Caitlin or Troy in six months," Blake begins. And before they can ask him why, he says, "I had reason to believe Troy was screw—cheating. I made the mistake of telling her. Since then . . . radio silence."

Blake isn't trying to impress the detectives exactly, but he would like them to know that he's got experience with homicide interrogations, that they don't need to bother with pleasantries. Or manipulative ploys. But they probably know this already. For a few months during his senior year of high school, Blake's face was recognizable to most residents of southern Louisiana, including the detectives' own Montrose Parish. The headlines didn't mention him, of course. That distinction had gone to his early-morning visitor, Vernon Fuller: Son of High School Football Coach Slain

IN APPARENT HATE CRIME. But Blake had been a featured player in the drama—the survivor.

"So neither one's been in touch since last night?" the bald detective asks.

"What happened last night?"

"This evidence you had," Hairpiece diverts. "How exactly did you . . . uh . . . *bring* it to Miss Chaisson?"

"I didn't say I had evidence. I said I had reason to believe."

"That he was cheating on her?" Baldy asks.

Blake nods. Nova's nicknames for the men have proven so effective, Blake realizes he can't remember the actual name of either detective.

"Right. But . . . what was it that tipped you off?" Hairpiece continues. "I mean, was it e-mails? Some kind of Internet thing?"

"I've got friends who work the casinos in Biloxi. A few of them came to me and said they saw Troy come in with different women and that it looked . . . more than friendly."

"So it was hearsay."

"The camera footage wasn't." The detectives both give him a blank stare, until he adds, "One of my friends works security at Belle Fleur."

"I see . . ."

What? You thought a guy like me would only have friends who dressed the showgirls?

"And so you showed her the footage?" Baldy continues.

"Nope."

"Why not?"

"She didn't ask to see it."

"Why's that?"

"Because she didn't believe me."

"But there was footage . . ."

"I didn't tell her about it."

"I'm getting confused," Hairpiece interjects, and his "confused" expression is so forced Blake has to work not to roll his eyes.

"I told her what I had been told. She didn't want to believe it, though, so I left it at that."

"And then you guys went radio silent for six months until last night . . ."

"No. Not until last night. I still haven't heard from her. Or Troy."

"Sorry. Just seemed like you were having a pretty important phone call when we walked up. Thought maybe she'd given you a—"

"That was one of her employees. Calling to tell me what happened. They're concerned for Caitlin, obviously."

"So what did she say happened?" Baldy asks, palms open, eyes wide. *The guy must have a community theater background,* Blake thinks. "We'd like to know as much as everyone else."

"Apparently Troy went into the gardening shed with some woman. Only the woman came out. She was covered in blood, carrying an axe. And there was no body in the shed." He gave them a mirthless smile. "Sounds like y'all might have the world's first axe-wielding illusionist on your hands."

He knows better than to ask them directly what the axe-wielding woman's story is, but he doubts they would tell him under any circumstances. His suspicions are confirmed when Hairpiece says, "Wow. *Someone* doesn't miss Troy Mangier."

"He's only been gone . . . what? A few hours? He'll probably turn up next to the river as soon as the sun's all the way up. Hungover. Again."

"Or bled out from an axe wound."

"Oh, I don't know. Troy always manages to land on his feet. Or Caitlin's back."

"So these friends of yours, the ones who work the casinos in Biloxi. They friends of Troy's too?"

"Not really. No."

"How'd they recognize him when he turned up?"

Blake curls his fingers around his Styrofoam coffee cup.

"Maybe you told them to be on the lookout 'cause you had some suspicions?" the detective presses.

Blake shrugs. "He was a gambler. With her money. She'd warned him about it. The women . . . those were a surprise to me."

"And Caitlin took his word over yours?"

"*No.* No, she . . . she didn't even bother to get his word first. She just dismissed me right on the spot and made all sorts of accusations."

"What kind of accusations?"

"The desperate kind." *And she used John's murder against me. And that was a rule between us—never use John's murder against me. And yet she broke it because she couldn't face the truth; she used it to hurt* me *to keep herself from being hurt.*

There was another reason the attack had caught him so off guard; he'd been braced for an attack of a different kind, a full-throttle version of the same half-assed accusation she'd always make whenever he became too protective or accused her of losing her head over some guy—that he didn't want anyone coming in between him and his access to what she often referred to her as her *incredible wealth*, which became even more incredible after the plane crash that killed her parents.

While the accusation was familiar, it was also absurd, and Blake would have been willing and able to defuse it in an instant, especially if he thought Caitlin's marriage was at stake. After all, he was the one who had repeatedly turned down her father's offer to give him long-term financial support if he took his daughter's hand in marriage.

Still, there was a small seed of truth to it. Over the years, Blake had taken great comfort in being a kind of adopted Chaisson, if not exactly a beneficiary. Without the Chaissons, he would have spent his teenage years alone, raised by vague memories of a mother who died when he was only four years old, a father who never managed to crawl out of the scotch bottle after losing his wife, and a passel of high-strung aunts from Dallas who popped in on a regular basis to make sure their brother hadn't made a complete mess of things. Meanwhile, Blake spent most of the major holidays with Caitlin and her family, and that had been just fine. More than fine, actually.

But he'd put himself through nursing school and paid his own rent while he did it. So he didn't owe Caitlin money or the kind of soft-glove treatment she was accustomed to receiving from her cousins and her late father's employees. He owed her the truth.

They allow Blake a moment to sip his coffee, then Baldy says, "Must not have been easy."

"Which part?"

"Making that kind of allegation against the cop who found your friend's killers."

For a while, nobody speaks. Blake watches the hummingbirds dancing in the branches on the other side of the plate-glass window. A few tables away an older woman cries into a man's shoulder, one hand still absently wrapped around her cup of tea in much the same way Blake is holding his cup of coffee. Blake recognizes them; their son was the overdose he treated sometime around 3:00 a.m. No telling how long that coma's going to last.

"John Fuller wasn't my *friend*, Detective."

Both detectives look startled for the first time since they all sat down together. Not by the information itself, but by the bristling anger with which Blake delivers it.

10

Willie Thomas lives in a tiny clapboard house hemmed in by a small forest of banana trees sitting just on the other side of Spring House's back property line. It is accessible by its own long private road, which means Blake can drop in on Nova without risking a run-in with Caitlin.

He's not quite ready for that.

After five hours of fitful sleep, every nerve in his body is still demanding that he reach out to his old friend. But he's known the woman for almost his entire life. Six months haven't changed her, he's sure. Any contact from him will be seen as an attempt to rub her nose in the sad truth about her husband, and that's the last thing Blake wants, especially if something terrible has happened to Troy.

So he vows to give her time. And space. Whatever that means. He doubts she's still at Spring House anyway. Unless the police have some strange reason to keep her there, and nothing about the detectives' questions that morning suggest they suspect Caitlin of anything other than having bad taste in men, he's pretty sure she's gone back to New Orleans.

While not quite confirmation, there's no sign of her on the drive out, no glimpse of her tiny gold BMW X 5 whizzing past him along the levee's gentle bends, and when he turns onto the mud-laced road that leads to Willie's house, the only person he sees is Nova, hurriedly stomping out a cigarette and tossing it over the side of the front porch.

"Really?" Blake asks her as soon as he steps from his Ford Escape.

"It's a clove cigarette," she says with the condescension of someone who has just enough college under her belt to think she knows everything.

"So what? Those are worse. And they don't even have nicotine, so you won't get a buzz."

She ignores this. "Caitlin went back to New Orleans."

"I figured. How's your dad?"

"Stitched up right. You want to check?"

"Did he go to a hospital . . . or did you do it?"

"You got me," she says, hands up in mock surrender. "I fixed him up with some alcohol and a little blowtorch."

"That's a really good school you're going to up in Baton Rouge."

Her smile is weak. Instead of inviting him inside, she holds the screen door open behind her just long enough for him to keep it from snapping shut in his face.

The tiny house is immaculate inside. He figures this is Nova's doing. Blake is not a regular here, but the few times he'd stolen a peek through the front door, it was clear Willie kept the house much the same way he kept his shed—every practical item within plain sight and easy reach, no thought at all to aesthetics.

Nova must also be responsible for the neat but prominent pile of textbooks placed on the kitchen counter. The featured title is *Africans in Colonial Louisiana: The Development of Afro-Creole Culture in the Eighteenth Century* by Gwendolyn Hall, and it's even angled slightly so as to be visible from her father's easy chair. It doesn't take Blake long to put together that the older and more educated Nova gets, the less comfortable she is with her father's marginally paid, codependent position at Spring House. These textbooks on the history of their people have the feel of AA literature left in the house of a hard-drinking relative.

"Iced tea?" Nova asks.

"I'm good. Thanks. Your dad?"

"Up at the shed. Cleaning up."

"Is that a good idea? It's a crime scene, isn't it?"

Nova turns to face him, one arm resting atop the refrigerator door she's just opened. "Crime scene techs went over it all night. Couldn't find a drop of blood inside."

"What? How'd it get all over that woman then?"

"Question of the day. And the next day. And the next . . ." She's staring at him expectantly, but he can't tell if she's letting this information sink in, or if there's something she wants him to do about it. It's not a hot day out and the open refrigerator is blasting cold air all over her, but Nova doesn't seem to give a damn.

"Who was she?" Blake asks instead.

"Some woman who worked with the caterer. Never saw her before."

"What'd she tell the police?"

"Nothing. She was just rocking back and forth when they took her away. Shock, I guess."

"Did they arrest her?" It's a trick question, sort of. The detective let slip that morning that the woman was still being held for questioning, which Blake took to mean *detained*. But Nova is being so evasive about what transpired here the night before, Blake hopes to draw her out a little by withholding some information of his own.

"For what?"

"Well, they'll have to test the blood, I'm sure. See if it was Troy's, right?"

"You know more about that kind of stuff than I do."

44

"Why'd you call me, Nova?" The question comes out more stridently than he means it to. But Nova Thomas is not usually this sullen and evasive, and her behavior is leaving him genuinely confused. And a little bit frustrated.

"Let's go see Daddy," she says, and then she's walking past him out the front door, Diet Coke in hand; she's avoiding his eyes now like someone trying to work up her nerve.

11

They walk in silence along the cane field belonging to the neighboring farm.

It is dusk and the tall, rustling stalks have rivers of deep orange snaking around their bases. When the plantation house and gardens come into view, it is the first time Blake has seen the place in half a year, and the nostalgia he feels in response startles and then overwhelms him, like a sharp poke in the side followed quickly by a passionate embrace from someone you've always lusted after.

There's the gazebo where he and Caitlin pricked their fingers and smeared the wounds together so they could become brother and sister for real. There's the grand oak tree, its heavy branches kissing the soil on all sides of its massive trunk, the same tree Caitlin's father hung a tire swing from for the two of them to play on as children. The idea that one of the tree's low-hanging branches might have been used to lasso slaves for the whip didn't occur to him until he was a junior in high school, and he wonders if it occurs to Nova now.

The house itself had been a ruin for the first six years after Alexander Chaisson bought it, and the children were forbidden to go inside, lest they crash through rotten floorboards or get crushed by a falling section of the roof. So the sprawling grounds outside became their private kingdom, and the gazebo their temple. Now there are flagstone paths and manicured gardens covering the expanse where decaying cane stalks once stood like the last timbers of a war-ravaged village. And the gazebo, which once seemed to be composed of as much lichen as wood, is a clean white shock against a canopy of banana trees.

"Are they starting up tours again?" Blake asks.

"Not for a week, Daddy says. Till all this dies down. You see any news crews on the way in?"

"Nope. Just some cop cars."

"They're searching an area close by for him. Least they were this morning. They think he might have stumbled a ways after she whacked him or something."

"But there's no blood inside the shed?"

He asks this again because he doesn't believe her, and apparently his tone makes that clear because she stops walking and glares at him over one shoulder.

She hasn't just stopped to stare, though, Blake realizes. She wants him to notice what she's standing beside. The fountain next to her is just a broad copper basin, one of the old sugar kettles that were part of the refining process. But the spigot has stopped running, and the basin is tipped so far to one side it's emptied all of its water onto the flagstone path. Blake tries to imagine someone lifting it. But the job would be too much for just one man. It would be too much for several men, especially if they were drunk, which most of the guests last night most assuredly were.

"Did the police do this?"

"Nope," Nova answers. "They didn't do that either."

She points to a spot where a planter has spit several of its bricks onto the flagstones. And *spit* is the best word he can think of for it. His first guess is that the earth underneath shifted and settled;

what was this land all around them but glorified swamp? But it can't explain the force that propelled the bricks out onto the path. A few seconds of blinking, and Blake realizes the only probable explanation is some sudden upward pressure. A heaving of some sort from below, and that's just . . .

"Nova, run to my truck, see if my shovel's—"

Willie Thomas has just emerged from the shed, when he sees who is standing beside his daughter in the lengthening shadow of the main house. And in an instant Blake watches Willie transform from a harried, overworked yardman to a smiling, happy servant whose every reaction to a white person is stained by a childhood of forced integration. As always, it is a transformation that makes Willie's only daughter bristle with a combination of anger and shame. Out come the huge, solicitous smile and the too-eager handshake, which Blake accepts because no matter how hard he tries to treat Willie Thomas as a peer, the man is determined to greet Blake from behind this protective mask of inauthentic good cheer.

"How you doing, Mister Blake?"

"I'm all right, *Mister* Willie. How you doing?"

"Oh, we jes tryin' to put things back together again, that's all. Miss Caitlin went back to N'Awlins, so—"

"I told him," Nova says.

"Well, that's fine," Willie says, but his emphatic nod can't distract from the icy look he's just given his only daughter. "This whole thing"—it takes some effort, but Willie puts the smile back on and focuses his attention on Blake—"this some misunderstandin', that's all. Mister Troy, he gonna come back soon. Five years married. I mean, they work through this. You see. They's jes no sense in everybody gettin' so worked up—"

"He's dead, Daddy."

Willie's eyes flash with anger; he's clearly been having this conversation with his daughter all day, and Blake wonders if the man agrees with her more than he's letting on.

"He's dead," Nova says again. "And we have no idea what killed him."

Before Blake can respond, Nova takes him by the arm and guides him toward the shed. "Come on," she says.

"Nova!" Willie calls after them. But his daughter is undeterred, and by the time she's pushed open the door to the shed, Blake feels Willie right behind them, breathless with anxiety.

Despite what Nova has told him, Blake is expecting a slaughterhouse inside. And so he is astonished by the cleanliness and orderliness before him. The only thing strange he sees is the set of indentations in the dirt floor. It helps that Nova has walked right up to them and has positioned the toe of her right sneaker next to the largest one. They have the appearance of rat holes, but the little dirt and debris piles you'd expect to find next to them are gone (although they were probably swept away by Willie's broom).

"Mower did that, Nova!" Willie cries.

"Lawn mower's been at our place for weeks. It was leaking gas all over, and Caitlin said she could smell it from the house."

"Something else then. I don't know."

"Rats?" Blake asks. He's standing right next to Nova now, and they are both studying the holes in the floor. There are five of them in all, and there doesn't seem to be a pattern or order to their spacing. And the dirt here is drier than most other parts of the property, which is why Willie chose this spot for the shed, so there should be some cracking or other evidence of the violence it would have taken to punch these holes. But there isn't.

"No evidence of digging," Nova says.

"You didn't sweep it away?" Blake asks Willie.

The man shakes his head and throws up his hands. "Mister Troy and that woman, they had some kinda crazy fight, and he stumbled outta here drunk as a skunk. Reason they can't find him is 'cause he's *not dead*. Now y'all come on outta here so I can—"

"That woman had so much blood on her it looked like she'd stuck a pig. And she would have cut you down with that axe if I hadn't stopped her."

"She was drunk."

"She was *terrified*!"

"Wait," Blake manages. "Everybody just . . . wait a minute. Are you saying there was something in here with them?" The silence startles Blake more than an affirmative response would. "So . . . you think something *punched* these holes down into the—"

"Not down," Nova says firmly. *"Up!"*

"Nova. What the . . ." It is the best Blake can manage, but the condescension ripples through even these basic, incomplete words. What is she saying? Some sort of animal punched up through a solid dirt floor and . . . what? *Ate* Troy Mangier, including the clothes on his back? It's a preposterous suggestion. The holes might be big enough for a snake or a rat, but nothing big enough to consume a fully grown man in an instant. But these thoughts aren't enough to keep a vein of heat from traveling up his right leg when he absently shifted his foot over one of the largest holes while Nova and her father were shouting back and forth at each other.

"Mister Blake doesn't need to be bothered with all your foolishness."

"I don't work for *Mister* Blake and you don't either, and he is here of his own accord, Daddy. And I know damn well you're not gonna tell him what you've been telling me about this place for years, so I'll just go ahead right now and—"

"Nova!"

50

"Tell him, Daddy. Tell him about the flowers, the ones we can't find in any book, the ones that don't die no matter how much poison you pour all over 'em . . . No? OK. Well, then I'll tell him about what *I've* seen. I'll tell him about the one you put in a pot on our porch, and then the next day it was gone. Not dead. Not withered. *Gone.*"

"Somebody picked that flower, Nova," Willie says, but he's resting one shoulder against the door frame, his glazed eyes studying the sunset as if it might be his last. It isn't resignation coming off Willie Thomas; it's defeat. Nova isn't lying; she is spilling secrets Willie has tried to keep for years.

"It's a private road, Daddy."

"What are you saying?" Blake asks. "You're saying the flower . . . *walked* away?"

"I'm saying something's not right in the ground here. We've all seen it—Daddy, me, the other staff—and we've all taught ourselves how to *un*see it. We're just like everybody else . . ."

"How's that?" Blake asks.

"So busy looking for ghosts in the attic, we never think to look in the ground."

Without so much as a sigh, Willie is gone, and for a few seconds, Blake and Nova listen to his footsteps crunching the ground outside the shed.

Blake feels a sharp pinch of sadness when he sees the expression on Nova's face: lips pursed and trembling slightly, glazed eyes focused on the floor. It is then that Blake sees the courage it took for Nova to make these insane statements, that despite her bluster and her anger, she believes every word of what she's said, and she is terrified . . . and now her father has abandoned her to Blake's skepticism.

He decides to be objective—as a nurse, it doesn't help in the ER to just make assumptions. As far as he can tell, Nova is not a drunk; she doesn't smell of weed. Her first few years of college have not produced the kind of wild tales of rebellion or self-destructive behavior that were common among most of Blake's friends when he was her age. And despite Nova's simmering resentment toward her, Caitlin used to update Blake on Nova's progress at LSU with a great sense of pride tinged with self-congratulatory noblesse oblige. Sleeplessness and the shock of watching her father almost get decapitated might be to blame for Nova's anger, but not the extent of her—he stops short of marking them as delusions, but honestly, what else could they be?

And where are the telltale marks of addiction and mental deterioration worn by so many of the raving lunatics Blake sees wheeled into his ER on a daily, sometimes hourly, basis? He doesn't see them, so he scours his memories of Spring House for any lost or buried recollection of walking flowers or strangely crawling vines. He finds nothing, but he also admits that his contact with the soil here is not as intimate as Willie's or Nova's, two people he has never known to tell a lie. If there *is* some strange, possibly supernatural secret to this place, it will be found in their memories, not his.

When he opens up his own memories, he sees himself as a child running the grounds fearlessly, convinced that he and Caitlin traveled beneath some bubble of adult protection that followed them everywhere. But the older he got, the more he came to fear jungles of shadows and open fields that seemed to lead to infinite darkness. The killing blow to his delusion of youthful invincibility was delivered by two assailants who attacked him and John Fuller one night during their senior year of high school. But truth be told, it was already dying before that awful night, and so for the past decade his experiences of Spring House have been confined to its parlors and guest bedrooms, not its gardens.

"I saw something . . . ," Nova finally says.

"What?"

"I knocked the woman down before she could kill Daddy. Then Caitlin was right behind me, and she opened the door to the shed. There was no sign of Troy. No sign at all. But there was something else . . . I don't know what it was, but it was low to the ground. About *there*"—she extends her foot until the toe of her sneaker is hovering above the spot in question—"and it was glowing."

"Glowing?"

"Yes. Glowing. Like one of those light sticks you get in emergency kits. Only it was different colors."

"What did the police say about it?"

"They never saw it. I don't know what she did with it."

"Caitlin, you mean . . .?"

Nova nods.

"What was it, Nova?"

She looks into his eyes for the first time in several minutes. "It was some kinda flower," she whispers. "And it was where her husband should have been. And everything about it was just . . . *wrong*."

Blake nods, more out of habit than agreement, then looks to the holes in the floor as if they might interject with a logical explanation of themselves.

"You don't believe me," Nova says. "Fine. I don't care. Here's the thing, though. We're *gone*. You hear me? We're gone and we're not coming back until you find out what that thing was."

"Does your dad know you're leaving?"

"Check the truck. His bag is packed."

"Jesus. Fine . . . But *me*? What do you expect me to do?"

"You're her best friend," she says, as if that is all the explanation necessary.

"I *was* her best friend. Six months ago. You think she's going to tell me anything right now?"

"Yeah, I do. It's not like she replaced you. No one else has the patience for her, I guess."

"Nova, if I call her right now about anything, especially *this*"—Blake stutters a bit when he realizes *this* includes crazy talk of walking, glow-in-the-dark plants—"she'll just think I'm trying to rub her nose in it."

"Then don't rub her nose in it . . . unless you think you won't be able to help yourself."

"Well, that's not fair. For Christ's sake, Nova, I'm a nurse, not a detective."

"And my father is not a slave!" she cries, whirling on him. "There is something dangerous here, and I don't care if she kicks him out of that house; he's not working another day here until I find out what it is. Now, he came close enough to death last night 'cause of some stupid white lady, and I'm not going to let it happen again, you hear me?"

"Nova, I know you've been mad at her for years, and I get it. Caitlin's behavior around your dad . . . it's not always healthy and . . . I get it, is what I'm trying to—"

"You don't know *anything* about my anger."

"Oh yeah. 'Cause I've never dealt with prejudice in my life."

"It's not the same."

"You're right. You didn't lose the man *you* loved."

"Not yet," she whispers.

And then she is gone. And Blake is left alone with the realization that in another minute or two it will be so dark outside he will either have to pull the chain on the lightbulb overhead, or leave the shed altogether. He chooses the latter.

12

A year before he died, Caitlin's father transformed one of the side porches of their home on St. Charles Avenue into a solarium, replacing its three walls of sagging screens with clean sweeps of plate glass. It is on the second floor and looks out mostly onto the neighbor's yard. Her father compensated for its oak-branch-filtered view of the Bickmores' swimming pool by lining it with potted plants Caitlin has done her best to tend since she inherited the house a few years before.

She can think of no better place to bring the flower she plucked from the spot where her dead husband should have been.

She has placed it inauspiciously in a tulip sundae glass, half-filled with water, and set it atop the white wicker coffee table beside a pile of unread copies of *Architectural Digest*, which she adds to once a month because the subscription is her mother's and she can't bring herself to cancel it.

For what feels to her like hours, she has been staring at the blossom, awaiting the return of the strange luminescence with which it first greeted her.

But the only otherworldly aspect to it now is its shape; the petals are too large, hand-sized, proportional to each other but not to its slender stalk. Their vibrant shade of white isn't bruised in the slightest, even after hours of being pressed against her flesh, hours in which she was questioned ceaselessly by the police, all the while wondering if the secret under her dress, the one laced under the waistband of her panties, was about to explode in another slick and thirsty eruption. Rather than frightening her, rather than quickening her words and making her appear sweaty and suspicious to the stoic detectives, this uncertainty filled her with a kind of delicious, drugged calm, and she wondered how many others found themselves drowsy and contented upon suddenly learning they were drifting through an upended world.

Even now, even in the absence of its strange pulses of light, she half expects the flower's supernatural promise to spread through the house, a reality-bending gas that alters the very fabric of each room. She wouldn't be surprised to see the regal portrait of her father in the adjacent sitting room suddenly peel free of its canvas and take a humanoid form, slowly dropping to the hardwood floor like a jewel thief suspended from a cable. If the patterns in the Oriental rug began to rearrange themselves into the alphabet of a strange new language, she would drop to the floor next to it and begin to take notes. In every dusty corner of the house, she can feel the possibility of upset and release, the low tremor of unborn energy.

Ever since she was a little girl, she has tried to nurse a belief in heavenly guardians; her bedroom was filled with framed pictures of cheerful cherubs and proud archangels, and for years little angel statuettes were everyone's go-to present when the time came to buy a Christmas or birthday gift for the girl who could afford to buy herself anything. But belief is a feeling and faith is a practice based in experience. Now she has faith; in her lowest moment, an angel did appear to her—only it had blossoms instead of wings.

Caitlin brings the flower to her nose and inhales. Its scent is something akin to charred sugar, sweet and smoky and a little cloying. Then comes a loamy undertone, an intoxicating compromise between turned dirt and the taste she'd often discover just below her husband's armpit during sex.

This smell of earth and flesh induces a state of feverish, sudden arousal; she finds herself going moist with the impossible speed depicted in the letters on *Penthouse Forum* she would sometimes read aloud to Troy when things had gone particularly soft in the bedroom. Is this response simply a result of being reminded of her husband? Her husband, who cheated on her at her own birthday party, just a few feet from where she stood. Her husband, who is now gone, gone, gone.

No. It isn't possible. This is a force greater than memory, and it is using her nostrils and mouth and sex as entry points.

The petals of the flower have rounded slightly around the edges, forming a half funnel that is now aimed directly at her. The stamens and filaments within have gone rigid, abandoning the slightly interlaced posture they've held since she first discovered the impossible blossom, and the slender stalk is curling gently back and forth through the water like a tethered tadpole.

The smell is gathering strength now—bread and semen and dirt lashed by rain and turning to mud—and with its growing power, a darkness is crowding in at the edges of her vision.

She feels her hand tense around the wicker love seat's arm. But when she looks down to make sure this isn't a trick played by the nerves in her arm, the hand she sees is black and callused. Her stomach lurches. The angle suddenly seems all wrong.

A name slices through her, as if it's been whispered in terror by a dozen guardian angels perched in the next room.

Virginie . . .

. . . When they take the blindfold off her, she sees they have brought her to a clearing where the trees are freshly splintered and some sort of foul-smelling chemical has been poured into hollows dug into their trunks. The horse beneath her shudders and takes several halting steps. On instinct, she jerks her bound wrists against her lower back, but it's no use. She is forced to steady herself by clamping her thighs down on the horse's flanks.

The overseer has his hand on its bridle, and he's staring up at her with as much fear as hate in his bloodshot eyes.

Beneath the light of a half-moon lies ample evidence Felix Delachaise's men have tried their hardest to turn the area around them into a desert. But in southern Louisiana, where land and water are often one and the same, it is not possible to make a desert even with the labor of a million men. But these men have tried. The mud looks plowed, roots torn up, perhaps by hand, only the shredded detritus left behind in a scrum that looks like sawdust.

She is, in ways she wishes she was not, startled by their bravery. They have seen only a glimpse of her power, when she brought the vine out of the oak to halt the overseer's whip because it looked as if Big John was near death from the flogging. For all they know, she could cause great roots to rise up from the soil and tear them apart.

And she could, perhaps. But it would kill her for sure, or cause a pain so bad death would be a mercy.

She speaks to the ghosts in the soil, and sometimes they need to be convinced. Coaxed. Charmed. And what is easiest for her is coaxing the fruits of the earth into quick and confident growth. Eruptions like the one she triggered the other day, the one that sent the overseer into a sputtering, red-faced rage, makes a pain like knives in her gut. But she can't let these men know that.

It takes her a few minutes of blinking into their lanterns and torches for her to count how many are there. The overseer and three men she doesn't recognize, probably white folks from a little ways downriver.

58

And then he steps forward into the light, Felix Delachaise, the master of Spring House. He has a forehead like one half of the temple roofs she's seen drawings of in stolen books, and his lips always appear to be peeling away from his face.

"No need for more fear at Spring House, witchy woman. Plantation life is hard on all of us. We are all a slave to the land here."

"Then, every now and then, we should all get the whip."

An angry shudder at her impertinence moves through the other men, but Felix just stares. It's a terrible risk, speaking to them this way, but she cannot let them know how severely they have limited her power by plowing this field. She cannot let them know how much it would require for her to unleash a true massacre.

"Don't remember you being punished so," Felix says.

"Don't much imagine I will be now."

"If you had the power of the Devil in you, you'd be gone by now, Virginie Lacroix. What makes you stay, working your trickery on my overseer?"

The very question she must avoid; to answer in any way would reveal the limitations of her gift, and oh, how those limits have caused her to lie awake nights cursing the God who gave it to her. Why? Why such a tiny drop of power and not the might needed to frighten the white man into seeing the Negro as brother and sister?

"Can't have no hanging tree when there's no trees," she says.

"No hanging is planned," Felix answers.

"Set me aflame then? Burn me like a witch?"

"Are you a witch?"

"They's ghosts in the soil. I can talk to them. That is my story."

"And you can make them dance. We've all seen that. Scared my poor wife half to death, that's for sure."

And there it is. His wife. She had seen some evidence of Virginie's gift over the years, seen the roses she'd brought back to life with a whisper and a touch. Kept the secret to herself as long as it gave her nice flowers.

But the other day, she'd been on the second-floor porch, watching Big John get whipped as if it were a nuisance on par with a mosquito in the bedroom, watching the great vine come free from the oak branches like a snake. And now Virginie is in the dark with men who rape her kind without a second thought. Men who have, at present, made no move to immolate or dismember her.

"What else can you do?" Felix asks, closing the distance between him and the horse that holds her a strange kind of prisoner.

"Kill me and be done with it," she says.

And then I'll let all hell break loose, 'cause I'll know I'm dying. I'll know for sure the pain won't last forever, *she thinks,* so I'll push it as far as I can, and I'll bring justice from the earth like the other slaves are always begging me to.

"*I have no interest in your death, Virginie. I have brought you here for other reasons."*

"Name them or be done with me."

"A trade, witchy woman," Felix says. "That's all. A trade."

Blake can see her from where he's standing on the front porch.

She's on her feet inside the solarium, her back to him and the broad, bustling avenue just beyond the house's fence. There is a strange, diseased-looking slouch to her posture, like she is staring down at something that threatens to draw her so far forward she will lose her balance.

He has texted her several times—for some reason this feels less intrusive than ringing her doorbell. He hates the thought that his brief, exploratory messages—*U OK? Do u need anything? U home?*—are what she's studying with such paralyzed intensity. The longer he watches her and the more she doesn't move, the harder it is for him not to ring the doorbell a second time. He gives in.

The doorbell is actually part of the intercom system, and after he hits the button on the brown box next to the front door, he's forced to stand there and listen to the gentle two-tone electronic chime that's now emanating from every telephone inside the house.

He steps back and looks up again. The house has always looked to Blake like a fat, sweating wedding cake. As a child he had recurrent dreams in which its dormers sloughed off like moist icing. Tonight it is lit up with its typical showplace precision behind the short decorative wrought iron fence that marks the quarter of a city block on which it sits, a proud landmark of the avenue, now sheltering a young woman who appears to be in the throes of some sort of nervous collapse . . . and then she collapses for real.

Years in the ER have familiarized Blake with the speed and intensity of her fall. The back of her hand does not flutter theatrically to her forehead; there is no last-second grab for any hard surface; up one moment, down the next. Total, stone-cold blackout that could be caused by anything from anemia to an aneurysm.

It is that same experience that springs Blake into action, the past six months of silence rendered irrelevant by a split second.

He is slaloming down the side yard of the house, past the concrete-framed swimming pool lined with enormous planters and crowned with a sleek chrome-and-concrete waterfall.

The kitchen and breakfast room have soaring paned windows that reveal the shadowed darkness within. With both hands he lifts the edge of a ceramic planter that once housed geraniums but is now filled with a multicolored arrangement of glass beads. His strength is considerable—it has been for years, thanks to an hour at the gym almost every day since John Fuller's murder, pressing and punching away memories of his killers. But the planter is heavy, and in the few seconds he has to risk using one of his hands to steal the spare key out from under it, the thing almost crashes back to the flagstones—and his fingers.

But he snatches the spare key up in one hand just in time. Then he's inside the house, not stopping to hit light switches, racing past the giant mural that covers one wall of the front hallway—Spring House in its glory, beneath a Maxfield Parrish sky of piled-high, purple-fringed clouds so detailed and luminescent that when they were seven, Caitlin was able to convince him you could see them moving if you looked closely enough.

Even as he races up the stairs, it strikes him how there is almost no evidence of Caitlin's husband anywhere to be seen. And it's not like she's had time to get rid of it. No, this is how the house has always been ever since Caitlin inherited it. It never felt to him like Troy was one of its rightful owners, more like a spirit that took up quiet residence in one corner of its master bedroom. And that presence hasn't lingered, even so shortly after his disappearance. But something else does, and it urges him onward, toward Caitlin.

He finds her on the floor of the solarium, facedown where he saw her fall, one arm pinned beneath her, the other twisted elbow-down. It's not until he has his hands on her, is rolling her onto her back, that Blake realizes she is shaking. Quivering, as if from a small but sustained electrical charge.

A seizure is his first guess, but none of the other telltale signs are there. The jerking isn't violent enough for it to be grand mal, and the timeline is all wrong; after this many minutes, she would be in the clonic phase, her arms and legs jerking sporadically, her facial muscles twitching to a different rhythm. He has seen plenty of seizures over the years, and the physical fits were more irregular than the steady full-body quiver that is turning Caitlin Chaisson into Jell-O.

He scans her for any further physical injuries, and aside from some light, rosy scars on her wrists—they look like day-old scratches left by plants—he can't find any. So he picks her up in both arms and carries her toward the bedroom, convinced the answer will be found in her medicine cabinet.

Her vitals are fine, her lips puffing as if she's trying to whisper something. The choked whispers sound creepy, but they also mean she isn't in danger of swallowing her tongue, so Blake chooses to see them as a comfort.

Caitlin has dabbled in various antidepressants over the years, but she's never been one for tranquilizers or painkillers, or any of the other highly addictive prescriptions people gobble like candy these days. The ones that might cause this kind of reaction.

He risks leaving her side for a second and scans the bathroom. But it looks untouched. The medicine cabinet doesn't have a fingerprint on it. He opens it anyway, and as the mirrored door swings open, it reveals Caitlin sitting upright on the bed, staring right at him with a glaze-eyed expression that says she does not find his sudden presence in her bedroom to be a surprise.

"A trade," she whispers.

13

"So . . . who did it?"

The three men have been standing inside the ruins of Fort Polk for a few minutes before Kyle Austin decides to break the silence between them. But the joke—if it could be called that—goes over like one of those old Lucky Dog stands in a hurricane, and then the three of them are armored in silence again.

Wind ripples across the still, swampy waters surrounding the decimated fort where they've chosen to meet for the first time in five years, and the crumbling brick walls give way to a night sky laced with low, fast-moving clouds. They're all staring down at the electric lantern on the dirt floor between them. Scott Fauchier brought the thing, and he's tried moving it around a few times but it's no use—every possible angle makes them look like Halloween ghouls.

"Not funny," Scott finally says. "Think about it. We've got no motive."

"Says who?" Mike Simmons asks, and Kyle marvels at how the man's solid teenage brawn has given way to layers of fat that rival Paul Prudhomme's. Suddenly he's imagining Simmons, former football team captain, barking orders at people while he zips around the carpeted offices of his little daddy-financed brokerage firm on one of those fat-people scooters, and he has to bury a laugh in the side of one fist.

Scott Fauchier, on the other hand, is just as tanned and pretty as he ever was, and he still has a tendency to bat his long golden eyelashes at the rest of them like a cheerleader in search of a date to homecoming. The three men haven't spoken much of their own volition, not since Troy Mangier tightened the noose around them when they were teenagers. But Fauchier's pretty mug has been impossible to miss. He's the poster boy for his own line of health clubs, which means he startles the hell out of Kyle at least once a week by popping up on the sidewall of a bus stop on Veterans Boulevard, shirtless and beaming and holding a folded jump rope over one shoulder as if it were hitched to a wagon full of old tires he was dragging without breaking a sweat.

"We stopped," Scott says. "The whole thing . . . he called it off as soon as he became Mrs. Chaisson. I mean, unless he made *you* guys keep paying. But the last time I—"

"You know, she's actually a pretty nice lady," Kyle interjects.

"Shut up, dude," Simmons growls. "Seriously."

"No, really. Katie was one of her maids when she was queen of Rex, and said she didn't let any of it go to her head. Said she was real sweet to every—"

"Will you *shut up*, Kyle?" Scott Fauchier says in a pleading tone that makes him sound like a teenager again.

But Kyle has already clamped his mouth shut. Not because of Scott's whiny request, but because just mentioning his wife's name in this secret spot feels like a dark violation. Like leaving her photograph up on the nightstand while boning a hooker in their bed. Which is not something he's ever done specifically, but he's done plenty else in his life. Otherwise he wouldn't be here in the hot, windy dark, one of three former high school heroes turned bitter, drunken slaves to their guilt.

65

When Scott Fauchier nervously licks his full lips, Kyle is seized by a jarring, nightmarish image inspired by a faggy prank e-mail one of his nurses sent him once, only now big fat Mike Simmons is the whip-toting, leather-clad freak in the bondage hood and full-lipped Scott Fauchier is the hairless, jockstrap-clad piece of oiled-up flesh, hog-tied at his combat boots. Amazing how badly the e-mail had gotten to him that day—he'd practically fired poor Lenny Jorgensen for sending it, which scared Lenny half to death. They sent joke e-mails around his veterinary practice all the time, mostly Photoshop jobs of Michelle Obama done up like some big-titted African villager. But never any kind of gay shit.

Never anything that made Kyle see John Fuller tied to the foot of that electrical tower again.

"Bitch is out of her mind," Fauchier continues. "That kinda money, it drives a person crazy. Just ask Simmons."

"Or lick my balls," Simmons snaps.

"No, seriously. I heard Henderson finally cut the cord and she's been like a shut-in ever since . . ."

Scott Fauchier realizes his mistake too late. He broke a cardinal rule; he said Blake Henderson's name aloud.

Now all three of them are remembering the way the kid sobbed and begged, not for his life but for John Fuller's. They're remembering how after they put the two men atop the concrete foot of one of the electrical towers and tied them back-to-back on either side of one of the tower's spindly metal legs, Blake Henderson started shaking his wrists violently. They're remembering how at first they thought he was trying to get free, and then they realized he was trying to shake life back into Fuller, who'd gone stone-cold after Simmons delivered the first, too-strong (un-*fucking*-necessary, if you asked Kyle Austin) blow from a lead pipe that was just supposed to be for show.

"My point is, it's been done, fellas," Scott says, his voice rendered a ragged near whisper by the force of memory. "It's been done for years. He didn't need our money anymore. Last payment was . . . when?"

"Five years, for me," Kyle says, even though he'd rather keep quiet now and watch the other guys slug it out, which has always been his way.

"Me too," Simmons grumbles.

"And me three," Scott whines. "So seriously . . . can we go now?"

"Yeah. That's it. We should just go," says Simmons, the one who had called them together, the man who, if you asked Kyle Austin, was ultimately responsible for everything going straight to hell that night. "The man who's got video of us leaving the scene of John Fuller's murder is either missing or dead, and we've got no idea who else has seen the film or where any of the copies are. But you're right, Fauchier. We should just take a fuckin' *wait-and-see* approach. Just let the chips fall—"

"All right, man. Chill. I didn't—"

"—where they fucking may. Or maybe we could just all act like the fucking feather from *Forrest Gump*, you know? Just drifting here and there and seeing which way the wind takes us."

"He's got a good point, though," Kyle says.

"Really? 'Cause I haven't fucking heard it."

"Five years, Simmons."

"And he could have started it right up again at any time. That greasy fuck had pussy up and down the Gulf Coast. It was just a matter of time before he got his dick snagged in one and Chaisson kicked him to the curb. This wasn't *fixed*, gentlemen. This wasn't *resolved*. We were never off the hook even after he stopped making us pay, and don't either of you forget it. Acting like we were . . . well, it's a little fucking reckless."

67

"Fine," Kyle relents. "Then what do we do?"

"Wait and see if Mangier was actually murdered?" Fauchier tries, feeling like it's his job to calm Simmons, given that it was his rush to get out of there that made him blow in the first place. "How's that sound?"

"Like shit," Simmons mutters. "That's how it sounds."

"OK, then . . . what?" Kyle asks again.

"Doesn't matter whether Mangier's dead or alive. One person's still around. And we need to know if she's seen the tape."

"Or if she knows where it is," Kyle says, nodding.

"Caitlin Chaisson?" Scott Fauchier asks, astonished. "You actually think she's part of this."

"What I think is that we need to watch her very fucking closely," Simmons whispers. "That's what I think."

"And how are we going to do that?" Kyle asks. And that's when his old friend looks at him with a level stare. The up-lighting from the lantern at their feet transforms the man's eyes into floating orbs guarding the entrance to deep, dark caverns in his skull.

"Glad you asked, Austin."

14

"It was just shock, I guess," Caitlin says.

"You didn't take anything?"

"There's nothing to take, Blake. Check the medicine cabinet."

"Did Willie make you a drink after the detectives left?"

"I can hold my liquor. I'm not fifteen anymore."

"But you did have a drink?" he presses.

"Yes, one drink," she says impatiently. "I'm not drunk, Blake."

"Anything weird to eat?"

She just shakes her head.

What he wants to ask, though, isn't about weird food. No, he wants to talk to her about the weirdness of seeing a strange woman swinging an axe that may or may not have been splashed with her husband's blood.

But they haven't gone there yet. They've been too busy playing out a similar version of this exchange over and over again, probably because the business of it distracts them from the strangeness of Caitlin's sudden awakening.

A trade . . .

For a few minutes, he'd actually held her in his arms before he realized she wasn't returning his embrace; her hands were pressed between their chests, and while she wasn't trying to pull them free, she reacted to the pressure of him with drugged resignation, as if he were an inevitable confinement following a criminal act. Now he is seated beside the bed, and she's staring vacantly at the ceiling. Blake is confident that if a long enough silence falls, the distance that grew between them over the past six months will once again seem as unavoidable as mortality.

Caitlin has rearranged the throw pillows on the bed behind her, and if it wasn't for her sporty outfit—a pressed polo shirt and skinny jeans—she would look like a princess greeting visitors from her deathbed. Her episode—whatever it was—has left her paler than usual, as well as glassy-eyed. A strange, uncharacteristic breathiness cloaks her every word.

"What trade?" It's the first time Blake has broached the topic of Caitlin's strange announcement.

There's no sign of confusion in her level stare. Just a tense calculation that doesn't match her next whisper: "What?"

"When you woke up, you said, 'A trade.' What were you talking about?"

Caitlin shrugs and shakes her head, but she's broken eye contact too quickly.

Is she embarrassed or frightened? He can't tell.

Suddenly she slides her legs to the floor and pads across the bedroom's plush carpeting. She draws the master bedroom's sliding double doors shut, one in each hand, stealing Blake's view of her father's old study across the hallway and the solarium just beyond.

"The detectives, probably," she finally answers. When she sees Blake's bewildered stare, she says, "I don't want the Bickmore kids staring into my bedroom."

It is a ludicrous statement, given the vast space between both houses, the preponderance of branches outside, and the distance between the bedroom and the solarium. But it seems the solarium is exactly where Caitlin still is. In her heart, at least, or her mind. Or in her strange, inexplicable dream.

He struggles to remember Nova's exact words. It was some kind of flower. And it was glowing and it was wrong.

"Did you see her?" Blake asks.

"Who?"

"The woman . . . the one with the axe."

"Jane Percival. Yes. I saw her."

"You knew her?"

"No. The detectives told me her name. I'd never seen her before in my life. Some friend of the caterer's or something."

"I bet that was . . ."

"What? You bet it was . . . *what*?"

"Hard."

"It was. It was hard . . ." Caitlin sits on the opposite side of the bed, her back to him, but he can see her face in the mirrored vanity a few feet in front of her. He can see both of them in it, looking awkwardly posed like the angry couple in some stock photo you'd find above an article listing the "Top Ten Reasons Marriages Fail."

"She was pretty," Caitlin whispers. "She's still pretty."

And this is the part where Blake is supposed to say, *You're pretty too*. And in response, Caitlin would turn to him, effect the grimace of a dying woman, and slur, *Am I still pretty, Momma?* Just like Angelina Jolie in that TV movie about the heroin-addicted model who died of AIDS, the movie that had rattled them both so badly when they'd watched it together in college they had no choice but to repeatedly mock its final, awful scene. But tonight this exchange, a convenient crutch they have always used to dismiss Caitlin's deep sense of self-loathing, strikes him as profane. Just another form of petty violence Caitlin can inflict upon herself for not being as beautiful as her mother.

These thoughts have taken him down a longer road than he intended to travel, and when Blake looks up, Caitlin meets his eyes in the mirror. There is a hard glint in her stare that sparks a bewildering surge of sexual attraction in him. Maybe because it is so uncharacteristically aggressive of her, so uncharacteristically *masculine*. He shakes his head, but can't quite dismiss the thought that Caitlin—*this* Caitlin—may not be the same person as his best friend from just six months ago.

When she speaks again, her voice has the hollowed-out quality of someone struggling to speak evenly through the breathlessness caused by fear. "He was fucking her. In the guest bathroom. Upstairs. The door was open and I could see him fucking her, and I . . . well, I guess I realized I don't have your courage, Blake. Or your mouth. I couldn't confront them, is what I mean. I just turned away and ran. And then . . ." Her tongue moistens her lips suddenly and quickly, an action that suggests her glaze-eyed stare is as substantial as a paper mask. "Then we all heard that little slut screaming, and then . . . Well, then it looked like there was more justice in the world than I previously thought."

Justice? He manages to keep this astonished question to himself, but the struggle must be written on his face, because Caitlin is studying him with sudden, animated intensity, and Blake realizes he is on the verge of failing an important test. Whatever he says next will determine her next move and the access she will grant to him until this whole thing is sorted out, to say nothing of his role in her life, if he's to have one at all, after this bloody affair has come to an end. She has assumed, without reservation, that her husband is dead, and he's confident that if she expressed this to the cops that morning as plainly as she just expressed it to him, they would still have her in holding.

He chooses his next words as carefully as he would insert an IV in an infant. "Nova said she saw something in the shed, right before

72

you went in." Blake scans the room for anything matching Nova's description of a strange flower that just isn't quite right, but he only sees the vanity bedecked with perfume bottles, and the nightstands stacked with paperbacks and copies of *New Orleans Magazine*. The sumptuous bedroom is still fresh from the housekeeper's last visit after Caitlin left for Spring House . . . but no flower.

"She wasn't sure what it was," he says. "But she said she saw it on the floor of the shed, and whatever it was . . . it was glowing. She thought it might be some kind of flower." His delivery at this point is sloppy and abrupt, he knows. But it is the quickest way he can think of to mask his stunned reaction to Caitlin's bloody definition of justice.

"She was probably drinking along with the rest of the *help*."

"So . . . no idea what she's talking about?"

"None," she says. "You're here because of something Nova said?"

"Of course not. I'm here because it's . . . *you*."

She doesn't turn to face him, but she is sitting upright, staring at him through the mirror, her hands clasped against her knees, her entire body braced as if she fears his next words might constitute a small, sharp strike to the center of her scalp.

"Do you think I killed him?" she whispers.

He wants to say, *No. You couldn't have.* But that answer is too logical, and it will reveal how thoroughly he's done his homework because of that very suspicion. Several witnesses placed her too far from the shed for her to have been involved in whatever took place inside. And he knows Jane Percival hasn't said anything to implicate Caitlin, and that if she had, Caitlin would probably be in an interrogation room with her lawyer at this very moment. Indeed, Jane Percival has said nothing the detectives want *anyone* to hear; she remains in custody, and there's no trace of her account in any of the increasing number of news reports about the bloody disappearance of a hero cop known for solving an infamous hate crime when he was just a Jefferson Parish sheriff's deputy.

"Of course not," Blake says. It is not his most convincing delivery, the words weighted down by forethought. But it's better than more hesitation, he figures.

Caitlin doesn't figure the same, because she says, "I appreciate you coming," yet there's anything but appreciation in her voice. It actually sounds like a dismissal.

"You thought I wouldn't?"

"I'd like to be alone now," she says, confirming his feelings, "if you don't mind."

Even though it was the impression he got in the first place, he is still surprised by how wounded he is by his curt dismissal, meted out, it seems, because he has refused to rejoice in the prospect that Troy might have been murdered by the same woman he cheated on her with.

"I'll call you tomorrow." And she is done with him.

"OK . . ."

His only exit is through the double doors, and when he recalls the speed with which Caitlin inexplicably drew them shut just a few moments before, he springs into action. Too quickly, apparently, because Caitlin senses he's got some agenda other than a hasty departure and begins calling out his name, her voice immediately shrill with fear.

"*Blake!*" she shrieks by the time he's passed through her father's study and is standing on the threshold of the solarium.

The flower isn't glowing, but there is a wrongness to it that makes him hesitate. At first Blake thinks it might just be its placement, all by itself in a sundae glass in the middle of the wicker table. But he's got plenty of experience not allowing a patient's paranoid delusions to change his opinions of needles and scalpels, and at the moment, that's exactly what Caitlin is—just another patient. And this is just a flower, he's sure of it. He closes the distance between him and the sundae glass and picks up the stem as gently as he can, given how quickly he's entered the solarium.

"Blake! Don't!"

In what feels like the same instant, Caitlin pulls him backward by one shoulder and slaps him across the jaw. Like an afterthought, the flower's stem slips from his right hand which has gone as slack as his jaw.

The shock is as total and paralyzing as that moment years before when it became clear the patch of darkness racing across the levee's crown toward the spot where he and John Fuller had been making out just seconds before was not, in fact, a trick of the eye, that it had arms and legs, that it was moving in a single direction with purpose, that it had a weapon.

Caitlin's slap seems to have unleashed a flood of adrenaline in her; she is bright-eyed and alive suddenly, after moving through what appeared to be a drugged fog, and once again a jolt goes through him, the odd attraction mixed with revulsion. And as the sting of her palm fades from his cheek like a muscle going lax, Blake confirms to himself what he had thought just moments ago: that while the woman standing a few feet away may have, at one point in time, been his closest friend in the world, she is now but a shadow of Caitlin Chaisson, a wavering reflection on moving water.

But there's no real comfort to this realization, just a cold vacancy inside that makes him dizzy. He is halfway down the front walk of her house when he hears her calling out to him. She's standing on the front porch, and as some young and tender part of him opens to receive her apology, she extends one hand and opens her palm.

"The key," she says.

He speaks before he measures his words, his sneakers slapping the brick walkway, and as he closes the distance between them,

Caitlin doesn't close her open hand or lower her extended arm, but her eyes widen in muted surprise.

"You were the first one I remember seeing," he is saying. "In the hospital room, when I came to. Before I could even remember what happened. Before they told me John was dead. You were there and you were holding my hand, and you were brushing my hair off of my forehead, and you were saying whatever you needed to say to keep me from going back there in my mind. That's how I know you didn't do it, Caitlin. Because you saw what murder does. You saw it in me every day for years. You can probably still see it if you look closely enough. Anyone can."

He's so focused on her expression that he's startled when her fingers graze his cheek. "Oh, Blake," she whispers. "All you know is flesh and bone."

These words hurt him more than her slap did, and he's not sure exactly why. When she plucks the key from his hand, he finds himself frozen in place and staring after her as the heavy front door drifts shut.

Caitlin Chaisson has been changed inexplicably by a sudden event that currently lies outside his realm of understanding, and this realization gouges him more deeply than any false accusation she might have leveled against him in the past.

15

Halfway home, Blake pulls his smartphone from his pants pocket and manages to scroll to the number for one of the detectives who interviewed him that morning, all without taking his eyes off the street.

He realizes, too late, he's programmed the man's name into his address book under "Baldy." Who the hell will he ask for if the number connects him to dispatch?

"Detective Granger," Baldy answers.

At least one of my problems is actually getting solved today.

"This is Blake Henderson."

"Good evening, Blake Henderson."

"Forgive me for asking this, but I don't suppose there's any chance I could talk to Jane Percival?"

"None whatsoever," the detective answers flatly.

"OK . . . Well, can't blame a guy for trying."

The silence on the other end startles Blake. He knew it was an inappropriate request, but he didn't expect the detective to be quite this offended.

"Blake . . ."

"Yes sir?"

"Get to a TV or a computer or something."

"Why?"

"You'll see . . ." And then the detective hangs up with the speed of someone whose partner or boss or wife has just walked in on him talking to a mistress.

A few minutes later, Blake is standing in front of the television in his apartment, watching the rebroadcast of the ten o'clock news on WWL. Watching Jane Percival's bagged body being carried out of the Montrose Parish sheriff's station by two medics who are bowing their heads as much as possible to avoid being captured by the cameras. This footage is juxtaposed with Glamour Shots of a strikingly pretty young woman with fine-boned features and huge, expressive blue eyes, a woman for whom suicide would be a vague and mildly troubling abstraction. And yet she is dead by her own hand, and—as the reporter explains—the blood found on her clothes the night before when she was taken into custody is the same blood-type as that of Troy Mangier. So apparently, despite her manicured good looks and broad, innocent smile, she is capable of murder as well.

A ruddy-faced, sputtering public information officer fills the screen, blinking nervously while he fields hostile questions from reporters about how long Jane Percival was questioned and how closely she was monitored and how she managed to get her hands on a piece of broken glass big enough to do herself in with. And Blake feels his hand reaching for the cell phone he dropped face-down on the coffee table in his mad rush to follow the detective's final instruction.

This time Detective Granger answers after the first ring.

"That was very helpful," Blake says.

"Uh-huh."

"And unnecessary."

"Yeah, well . . . Are you a man of faith, Mr. Henderson?"

"Not really. No."

"Because of what happened to you?"

"I have faith in certain *things*. But . . . man of faith. It just sounds a little broad, to me, you know?"

"You're not friends with any reporters, are you?"

"My experience is they don't make very good friends."

"Uh-huh . . . And the friends you do have? Spent any time with them lately?"

"Caitlin Chaisson?"

"Yeah."

"I was with her earlier."

"So you're going back out there?"

"Spring House?"

"Yes. Spring House."

"Sure . . ." *I'll let you think I'm headed there right now if you fess up and tell me what's eating you, Detective.*

"If this gets back to me, I'll deny it. Like standing on my momma's grave deny it. And then I'll find you and beat the shit out of you, get me?"

"I got it." *Cop bluster. So typical—and such a waste of time. Just tell* me!

"The vines . . ." Blake waits for the man to finish, but he's been left with the ticking sound of his old refrigerator. He's turned the volume on the TV down, but not too much, so that the news report on a fire at an apartment complex in Gert Town is a low murmur.

"Detective?"

"She said the vines did it. She said the vines are coming for us all."

There is just enough sarcastic bite in the detective's tone to suggest he's repeating these words the way he might repeat the ravings of a homeless woman who accosted him on his way into his favorite watering hole. But he's still repeating them, and that fact alone renders Blake speechless for a moment.

"Is that all she said?" Blake asks.

"Yep. Fifteen hours we held her . . . and that was the only thing she said the whole time. But she said it the *whole* time."

Then Blake hears the dial tone, and he feels something deep within his bones that he can only describe as a shudder. It returns him to a childlike state of conviction that darkness itself is a substance with the power to rise up around the edges of any place and claim it with the sudden finality of a whale's mouth closing over a drift of plankton.

More frightening to him than Caitlin's slap earlier that evening, the phantom after-burn of which Blake can still feel across his jaw, is Granger's willingness to share information pivotal to an unfolding PR nightmare for his department.

He was warning you, Blake realizes. *That's why he asked you if you were going back to Spring House anytime soon. He may not believe there's something out there. But he believes Jane Percival believed it.*

The detective was scared, and in Blake's experience with cops, that meant he should be scared too.

Nova answers her cell phone right at the moment when Blake fears he's about to get sent to her voice mail.

"Where are you?" he asks.

"Hello to you too," she says.

"Where are you?" he repeats.

"Calm down, Blake. I'm in Baton Rouge."

"School?"

"In the morning. Right now . . . research."

"Research?"

"Yep." But that's all she says.

"Meet me in Gonzales. It's halfway."

"Now?"

"Jane Percival killed herself tonight. If you want to hear what she said before she did it, meet me in Gonzales. Then you can tell me about your *research*."

"Gonzales . . . I'm not sure I like this game."

"I'll come to you if you want." The way he says it, it is either a desperate concession or a veiled threat.

She apparently doesn't want to risk it. "All right, all right. Gonzales it is. What, like, a . . . gas station?"

"There's a Waffle House."

"A Waffle House . . . I thought the gays liked to eat at nice places."

"Commander's Palace isn't open this late, OK? So . . . Waffle House?"

"Yeah huh."

Blake is about to hang up when a thought strikes him. "Nova. Where's your father?"

"With my aunt in the Seventh Ward."

"Good."

16

Caitlin has returned to the solarium in darkness, where the blossom's white petals are still visible in the branch-filtered glow from the streetlight on the nearby corner. The flower no longer gives off the loamy scent that knocked her out of her body and into a tortured fragment of Spring House's secret history. But perhaps she's standing too far away; perhaps if she leans in a little farther, its filaments will once more grow erect and more of its secrets will penetrate her fevered mind.

Out of the corner of her eye, she can see a shadow dart down the side of the house below. Her first thought is that it must be Blake. That he's come back to snatch the flower now that he thinks she's asleep.

But if he's going to break in, he'll have to do it the messy, old-fashioned way. After he left, Caitlin tested the key to make sure he'd returned the right one, and then she'd cast the house in darkness with the press of a single master switch next to the back door. For a while, she'd sat on the stool just inside the foyer, listening to the clatter of passing streetcars and briefly paralyzed by the realization that her encounter with forces from beyond this world hadn't rendered her immune to the guilt and remorse her old friend could stir in her by just cocking his head to one side. But just seeing his fingers close around the flower's stem felt like a violation close to rape, and what choice did she have? When dark miracles suspend the rules you once lived by, you have no choice but to let your feelings be your guide, no matter how extreme they might seem to others.

In an instant the intruder has disappeared around the back of the house, where, she assumes, he is trying to get a good look into the breakfast room. For several breathless minutes, she awaits the soft shatter of glass or the sound of tools prying at a lock. But the house is silent, save for the ticking of the grandfather clock in the upstairs hallway.

Blake has had years to make a copy of the key to her house. But something about this theory feels flawed, and so she finds herself padding swiftly into her bedroom, where there is a gun in her nightstand drawer. It's Troy's gun, but she knows how to use it.

She has pulled the gun from the drawer and unsnapped its holster when her iPhone vibrates softly on the nightstand. The text message is from Blake.

Jane Percival killed herself.

Caitlin is less stricken by the content of this message than she is by the realization that it's highly doubtful Blake would have tapped it into his phone while trying to sneak into her darkened kitchen.

She raises the gun in both hands and starts for the hallway. More silence from the vast house. She returns to the solarium. She half expects the flower to recoil from the sight of the gun alone. They're connected now, aren't they? She and this strange dream-giving blossom. Its absence of a reaction disappoints her, a small but cold rejection after it graced her with its life-altering scent.

Below, the shadow darts past the pool, bound for the back fence. The apparent senselessness of this move infuriates her. She was oddly more comfortable with the idea of someone breaking in and trying to kill her. But now the intruder's motives seem unknowable.

Why make an escape over the back fence when he could just as easily sweep down the side of the house and over the decorative little wrought iron gate in front? If he's a burglar, why did he bypass the cabana, which had things of real value inside?

Again he appears, this time on the other side of the pool. She can see he's hunched over now, holding something in both hands. Some sort of hood or stocking cap covers his face and head. And he is fat, his movements hurried, but ungainly. There's no bag or backpack, nothing in which to hide a cache of stolen goods. And now he appears to be headed for the garage.

The back fence, she thinks. *What the hell was waiting for him at the back fence? Why did he hang out there for a good five to six minutes? What's at the back fence other than a view of the house?*

A view of the house . . . No bag for stolen goods. Pausing briefly at various points throughout her backyard, where there's nothing of value to steal . . .

The police don't work this way, not even in New Orleans. And as Caitlin turns it over and over in her head, she can think of only one explanation for the guy's strange zigzag path through her property. He is after views. He is after angles.

He is planting cameras.

There is a purity to the rage that courses through her now. It is not the feeling she expects; it has nothing to do with having her privacy invaded. It has more to do with the realization that if someone other than law enforcement is placing her under surveillance now, there can only be one reason: Troy.

How many other deceits were woven through Troy's infidelities? How many gambling debts or hidden bank accounts? As a freshman in college, she'd been stricken by a public-health notice in her dorm that assured all who read it that when a patient tested positive for one sexually transmitted disease, they were likely to test positive for another. Surely this was just as true when it came to diseases of character.

Before she has time to reconsider, Caitlin pulls the letter opener out from the stack of mail pinned beneath the magazines still sent every month to her dead mother. She presses the tip against the flesh of her palm, then gently presses upward until she feels a slight tug that tells her she's cut the skin. Then she presses harder, until a thick vein of blood emerges from the center of her palm.

She expects the blossom waiting below to expand its petals, to raise its stamens with evident and undeniable thirst. But the flower does no such thing. Indeed, the first drop of blood hits the white petal and rolls off it like water on a Scotchgarded sofa cushion. The petal isn't even stained. In a panic, she wonders if it's a simple matter of volume, remembers the arterial flow she'd opened from one wrist the night before. There's no way she can risk that again, not now, not here.

The pain in her palm becomes unbearable. She drops the letter opener and dives for the love seat, then brings a wad of tissues to her bleeding hand. They are soaked through in seconds, and she is left with the gun, and the oblivious blossom that lacks the same thirst as the vines that gave it life, the vines that snaked up through the floor of the gazebo and nursed from her mutilated wrist. It is a wholly different thing. And that makes sense, doesn't it? Whatever strange force animates them, these are living things, and like all plants, they possess various phases of thirst, growth, and bloom.

Below, the shadow now saunters through her backyard. The man—she's reasonably sure it's a man—looks back over one shoulder, lifts his arm, and waves in the direction of the back fence, and that's when Caitlin's suspicions about the guy's intentions are finally confirmed. The yard, the back door, the garage—she's confident all are now under surveillance. And the slow, arrogant swagger this bastard has acquired during his nighttime visit to her property fills her with fresh rage.

If the flower before her wasn't equipped to come to her rescue, perhaps it was time to visit its source.

When she hears the *tap tap tap* against the glass next to her, she's willing to believe that the stranger has floated up to the second story of the house and is rapping against the solarium walls with one fist, and she shoots to her feet, gun in one hand. But instead of a floating shadow, she finds herself looking at the streetlight on the corner through some kind of black gauze. But gauze isn't the right word for it. More like cheesecloth that's been pulled over the entire sheet of glass—only the gaps in it are shifting and rearranging.

Bugs. They've lined the outside of the glass wall with such intricacy and precision that it's hard for her to see them as anything other than graceful, and so referring to them as bugs seems like an insult. There are so many of them, so densely packed, that she can't tell what exact type they are, only that there is more than one kind. She has spent most of her life living in fear of palmetto bugs, what people refer to as the classic New Orleans cockroach. But if they're among this strange legion, they're too outnumbered to strike a primal chord of fear in her.

She places her free hand against the glass, even knocks a few times. No response from outside. Then she places the gun down and lifts up the sundae glass carefully in both hands, and as soon as the blossom's giant white petals are a few inches from the glass, a great pulse moves through the swarm outside. The streetlight is blacked out completely as the lace pattern suddenly gathers into a solid cluster of rustling darkness, a black halo around the spot where the blossom is kissing the glass.

Caitlin's laughter is a warm, rich thing, a mixture of arousal and delight as sensuous as the sounds Jane Percival was making in the upstairs bathroom at Spring House while Troy fingered her.

She sets the sundae glass down on the end table right next to the window, and the swarm pulses again. The borders shift, but it holds its general shape even as it moves several inches down the glass to be closer to the flower.

It occurs to Caitlin that just a few days ago, this sight might have horrified her—this sight *should* horrify her—but now her cheek is resting against the glass, her fingers tapping gently in time to the sounds of more and more insects pelting the thickening blanket of cicadas, flies, moths, and palmetto bugs. Now Caitlin feels embraced by hidden forces laced through soil and sky. And she feels comfortable leaving the blossom behind as she returns to the patch of Spring House that gave birth to it. If the insects assembled on the other side of the glass are not her protectors, there's a good chance they will act as guardians to the flower that drew them out of branches, gutters, and nests. At the very least, there should be enough of them by the time she gets back to completely hide the solarium from view.

17

"She's leaving," Scott Fauchier says. "He's gonna follow her."

"Ask him about the bugs," Kyle Austin says.

"The what?"

"The *bugs*. Look!"

Kyle points to the giant computer monitor on Scott's desk, and suddenly Scott is bending over so close to him Kyle can smell the bergamot in his cologne.

Scott's loft-style apartment is inside an old brick school building on Magazine Street, a few blocks from the Mississippi. The furniture is all glass and steel, the carpets a dull shade of gray that looks like it wants to turn into a deeper, richer color. Everything about the place screams Miami coke dealer, and when Scott offered him something to settle his nerves, Kyle was surprised he didn't have anything stronger than Grey Goose. There are pictures of grown-up Scott everywhere—usually with a buffed-up, ponytailed little trainer on his arm—but the way the two of them have been lounging in front of the computer for most of the night, waiting for Mike to set up the wireless cameras, has made Kyle feel like a teenager all over again. The thought gives him a warm fuzzy feeling and he actually smiles, before he remembers he and Scott had sort-of murdered someone when they were seventeen, and that was the only reason they were hanging out at all. That's what guilt truly is, Scott realizes, a fishhook's tug on the third or fourth minute of every happy moment.

"You see 'em?" Kyle asks. His finger is hovering several inches from the spot where what looks like a swarm of moths are dancing in and out of the streetlight's exaggerated green glow around one corner of the second-floor solarium.

"Fuckin' bugs, I don't know," Scott says. "What are we? Her exterminator?"

But Scott lifts the prepaid cell phone Mike bought for them earlier that night to his ear and repeats the question. He listens for a few seconds, then says, "He's gone. Says he didn't see any bugs. Can we stay focused on what's important?"

"OK," Kyle says, holding back his anger. "Tell me again . . . what's important?"

Instead of answering—your wife, my line of health clubs, my endless succession of well-muscled girlfriends—Scott pads across the expansive apartment toward the bottle of Grey Goose sitting on the kitchen counter.

18

Nova's battered Honda Civic is parked outside of the Waffle House between two pickup trucks. The car's back window is a bubbled mess of lamination film, and the LSU bumper sticker is mud-lashed and frayed at the edges.

Before he passes through the front door, Blake spots her sitting at the counter alone, slumped over a spread of papers and file folders. The portly waitress refilling her iced-tea glass has wide eyes and pencil-thin eyebrows that give her an expression of restrained panic even as she greets Blake with a casual nod.

When Nova looks up at his approach, Blake sees the tense set to her mouth, the way her right hand has curled into a claw atop the papers she was just reading. He wonders if she was willing to make the forty-minute drive here from Baton Rouge because she doesn't expect to sleep anytime soon.

For a while they just sit next to each other on their respective stools as trucks lumber by outside, bound for the I-10 on-ramp. Blake wonders if moving to one of the empty booths nearby would strike Nova as too intimate, too forced.

"I know why you hate her," he finally says.

"Caitlin?"

"Yeah."

"I don't hate her."

Nova is collecting the pages in front of her, arranging them in a neat pile as if she planned to shove them into the purple backpack at her feet but then remembered they were part of the information-sharing deal she made with Blake earlier that night.

"Fine. I know why you're mad at her."

She gives him a blank stare, as if there's nothing she likes less than having her mind read by white boys.

"I remember . . . It was last year, right after her parents were killed. Your dad said something to me about how he was putting the money together for his own landscaping business . . . " Nova looks away suddenly. He's scored a direct hit. "He said he and his brother were going to team up, maybe try for a bank loan. Then I never heard anything about it again. Caitlin . . . She killed it, didn't she?"

"She offered him the house."

"So . . . kind of a fair trade."

"A trade? How? He lives there, but he doesn't own it. And she pays him *less* now 'cause of it. He's got no insurance, and now has to ask her every time he goes to see a doctor. It embarrasses him. He won't let her see it, of course, but it does. He . . . he could have started something of his own, you know? Something with his name on it. But the minute she gets wind of it, she starts screaming and crying like she's about to lose her parents all over again. Like he's *her* daddy and not . . ." *Mine.* The word, unsaid, hangs in the air between them like a cloud of cigarette smoke. "All so she didn't have to hire a new yardman."

"He's more than a yardman."

"In your eyes, maybe. But he doesn't get paid more than one."

"You know what I mean."

"I do. And you're wrong. We're not her family. We never have been. We've worked every party she's had. We've never been guests. Not once."

She has spoken a truth about their position at Spring House that he acknowledged silently to himself a long time ago, and then rationalized away with glib self-assurances that Willie and Nova felt included and somehow affirmed by the company of wealthy white people.

It also dawns on him that, despite their pact in the gazebo as children, he isn't necessarily family either. Caitlin's slap earlier that night was proof of that. Maybe if he'd accepted Alexander Chaisson's insane offer when he was fourteen, they would all be better off. Maybe he and Caitlin would be trapped in a loveless marriage defined by self-loathing and deceit, or maybe not. Maybe they would have worked out some mutually beneficial arrangement. Maybe he never would have fallen in love with John Fuller ,and Caitlin never would have been betrayed by Troy. Or maybe his thoughts are now as crazy as Caitlin's recent behavior, and he should consume something that isn't mostly sugar or caffeine.

"Are you all right?" Nova asks.

The effort it's taken not to laugh at his inane speculation has left a strained half smile on his face that probably makes him look drunk, which is exactly what he'd like to be. "Booth?" Blake asks.

Nova nods, collects the papers in one hand, then hooks the strap of her book bag with the other. They cross the tiny restaurant together, heads bowed and brows furrowed, as if they're doing so at the order of a demanding school teacher.

Once they're sitting across from one another, he can see what her profile didn't reveal: eagerness, anxiety, a desperate need to have her fears confirmed. After all, she was the one who gave him the order to infiltrate Caitlin's home in search of some impossible blossom.

The flower he tried to grab didn't quite fit Nova's description, but Caitlin's behavior was stranger than any otherworldly plant.

When Nova senses his hesitation, she says, "I'm sorry about what I said . . . about John."

Blake is startled into silence by her use of John's first name. As far as he knows, Nova never met or laid eyes on John Fuller. She was just a girl when he was murdered, and his relationship with Blake—their secret trysts and desperate make-out sessions; those late nights when John would call Blake and not say anything, just play that new Faith Hill song everyone was so crazy about into the phone; their fumbling sexual experimentation in the shadows of the Lake Pontchartrain levee just a few blocks from Blake's home—had no public face until after John's murder.

"What did you say?" he asks.

"The thing about losing the man you loved. It was . . . it was probably more than I should have . . ."

"It's just the way you said his name. It kind of caught me off guard is all," he whispers.

"We went to the funeral. I remember, 'cause Daddy took me out of school."

Blake is sidelined by this, more so than by Caitlin's precise slap. He tries to recall the rows of mourners packed inside the Unitarian church John's mother had been forced to pick for the service. While there was a good chance her parish church would have overlooked the facts of the case and given her son a proper Catholic burial, by then Deborah Fuller had become an unlikely and hastily assembled gay rights activist whose every public move was scrutinized by a variety of national media outlets. She and Blake were clinging to each other for support every time the cameras swung in their direction, each shot giving credence to the illusion that Blake had been a son-in-law and not a secret.

Now Blake scans the rows of mourners in his memory, searching for a younger, leaner Willie, clean-shaven and muscled as he was in those days, and his bright-eyed young daughter, her hair fastened in two matching braids. Perhaps they were jammed in the back somewhere, or perhaps his memory isn't what it used to be, because he doesn't see them. And he can't recall the funeral with the same clarity with which he sometimes dreams it. All he sees are the stunned faces of his fellow students . . . and Vernon Fuller—John's father, Coach Fuller, as he was known to all of their classmates—practically curling into a ball, reeking of bourbon, retreating silently yet entirely from the media spotlight and its incessant demand that he publicly accept his son's secret life with as much chin-up determination as his wife.

Blake tries to take a breath, but it feels as if his nostrils have been plugged once again with the gauze he woke up with the night of the murder. And then he is blinking back tears, and Nova has bowed her head at the sight of them.

These are the moments when the sense of loss sneaks up on him. He can spend hours lighting candles at John's mausoleum, engage in all manner of planned rituals designed to purge himself of sadness, and the tears won't come. Rather, it is in these moments of fatigue and distraction that the grief overtakes him. He knows it's childish, but there is a belief in him that ever since that terrible night, his is a life half-lived, a desiccated alternative to the fantasies he and John whispered as they held one another on grass kissed by hot winds off the lake. Who cares if the life they plotted for each other once they were free of high school had been nothing but teenage fantasy, devoid of accountability or consequence? That lesson should have been theirs to learn.

"I didn't know you were there," he manages quietly.

"We were in the back. Daddy, he thought it was *important* that we went. Not just for you. But 'cause the . . . you know, so people could see . . ." There's a bitterness in her voice now, and after a few seconds of tasting it, Blake is able to identify its source. Nova's father wanted them at the funeral because John's murderers had been black.

Delray Morrison and Xander Higgins. Their mug shots are emblazoned in Blake's memory with greater clarity than the funeral. Blake had sensed the presence of another assailant that night but he hadn't seen one with his own two eyes. In light of the head injuries he'd suffered during the attack, he wasn't willing to cast further doubt on his testimony by insisting on the presence of a ghostly third attacker. Besides, the evidence that Morrison and Higgins had acted in concert was almost impossible to argue with.

It was Troy Mangier, then a young Jefferson Parish sheriff's deputy, who had thought to look into several attempted carjackings in Jefferson Parish reported in the weeks before the murder.

Barely a week after John was killed, Troy pulled over two young black men who were carrying materials in their trunk that matched the bindings used to lasso John and Blake to the foot of the electrical tower. The brazenness of this, cruising through the same part of town where they'd committed a deadly assault just a few nights before, would be used by the prosecution to paint both men as remorseless killers.

But they pleaded their innocence until the very end. Didn't even try to go for a lesser charge. Didn't try to convince the jury that John's death had been unintentional. Just kept saying it wasn't them.

And in a way, they hadn't been lying.

After all, it was the water that had really killed him. The water that had risen around them with the silent determination of smoke filling a room.

Technically, John Fuller's murderer was a pumping station, a nondescript one-story white building that plugged a hole in the levee where one of the drainage canals dividing Jefferson Parish entered the lake. You weren't supposed to swim in Lake Pontchartrain; the water was too polluted, and boats didn't launch from that spot, so almost no one—not even the affluent white families that lived just on the other side of the levee's green rise—were all that familiar with the exact rise and ebb of the water along the rocky shoreline, particularly after dark.

The autopsy suggested John's head injury was so severe he might have wound up in a coma even if Blake had been strong enough to free him before he drowned. But it didn't matter. The feel of the rope through his desperate, prying fingers, the weight of John's body, all of it thrummed within Blake like a second heartbeat as he spent hours in the gym, turning himself into a tower of muscle that at present was just shy of cartoonish and a few years away from grotesque.

Delray Morrison. Xander Higgins. They'd made the mistake of forcing a lousy public defender to try to prove they were never there at all, and they'd lost. And now they were dead. One shanked in the prison yard, the other dead of a drug overdose in his prison cell.

Now they seem to hover over the table between Blake and Nova like entangled spirits, and Blake wonders if this is sign of growth on his part, that he can actually feel concern for how Nova might feel that the men who murdered his first boyfriend were black.

"Nova . . ."

"What?"

"You know, I don't . . . That I never . . ."

"You never what?"

Never held it against you? Your race? How could he say that without sounding like a complete ass? How many times he gritted his teeth in anger over the years when his devout Catholic colleagues would say things like, *You're not like those* other *gays, Blake.* And *his* people hadn't been enslaved for hundreds of years.

"It means a great deal to me that you were there," he finally says. "That's all . . . It means . . ." She's watching his face intently, but she's withdrawn her hands from the edge of the table as if she fears his emotions might require a small seizure to get free.

"So," she finally says, "I take it things didn't go so well with Caitlin."

She's waited a respectful amount of time to say them, but her words still feel like a dismissal. Is she as uncomfortable with forced moments of so-called understanding between races as he is?

"She slapped me," Blake finally says. He feels strangely as if he's just betrayed some sort of confidence, and it gives him a slight taste of what abused spouses must sometimes feel.

"Why?"

"Because I tried to take it with me."

"The flower?" Nova asks, sitting forward, as bright-eyed and eager as he's ever seen her. "It's there? You saw it?"

"It wasn't glowing. But whatever it was . . . it didn't look right. Out of proportion. Strange. I don't know . . . What matters is she didn't want me going anywhere near it. Listen, I went online before I left the house, and there are all types of hallucinogenic plants out there. But not the kind you can just get exposed to. You have to either eat them or smoke them or—"

"You think I *hallucinated* it? You just saw it yourself."

"Yeah, I did, and it wasn't glowing. So maybe it's mind-altering in some way if you're exposed to it in—"

"I saw it for thirty seconds through a door. I didn't touch it, didn't smell it. My daddy was closer, and you heard what he thought when I talked about the flower. I wasn't hallucinating, Blake."

"Fine, but maybe Jane Percival was when she killed Troy."

"Then where is Troy's body?"

"I don't know."

"So you're gonna blame Caitlin's crazy on some flower that's making her hallucinate? You think that's why she slapped you?"

"I think she's falling apart. I think she's been falling apart for a while—since even longer than all this started—and there's not much I can do about it."

"Kinda hard to blame a *flower* then, isn't it?"

Blake has no response to this. Finally he points to her pile of papers. "Your research?"

Nova chews her bottom lip for a second. He figures she wants to press him for Jane Percival's last words. But he's already given her an intimate look inside Caitlin's home and deteriorating mental state. It's quid pro quo time, and he isn't budging.

"So Spring House allegedly burned down in 1850—"

"Wait a minute. *Allegedly?* Felix Delachaise got wasted and burned it down because he was broke. He couldn't manage the fields. An entire cane crop died on him, and he lost his shirt. Didn't his whole family die in the fire?"

"Allegedly. There are those who claim something else happened—something that had nothing to do with Delachaise and booze."

"So, wait. The family survived?"

"No. I'm saying they might have been killed by something more than a fire."

"OK . . . And who exactly believes this?"

"The slaves who fled that night."

"I see. So you found them all on Facebook?"

She rolled her eyes. "Close. Dr. Taylor found them on the Internet, in a manner of speaking, that is. She's one of my professors at LSU. She's working with a couple other universities to create something called the Lost Voices Project. It's the most extensive database on African American slaves ever built."

"What is it? A list of names?"

"Oh, it's *a lot* more than that. There's a professor down in New Orleans, Gwendolyn Hall, she went into old slave auction records and put together an exhaustive list of slave names and identities. Dr. Taylor, she's building on top of that kind of research. Only all sorts of information goes into the system. Slave narratives taken before and after the Civil War. Diary entries from plantation owners. Travel logs, newspaper reports from the period. All of it gets filtered through algorithms and computer software that work to assemble a complete reconstruction of every slave. I mean, even down to their physical appearances, their mannerisms, their speech patterns. The eventual goal is to have a database where you can actually sit there and have a conversation with a slave. But that's years away."

"Virtual slaves . . ."

"Virtual *ghosts*. Back from the dead. Folks whose lives were ignored and tossed aside in the history books. Now they're coming back to life 'cause of the kind of computer software that tracks what you buy on the Internet." Nova's excitement over her professor's vision has *her* excited, straight-backed, and talking with her hands. She catches herself with a quick but deep breath and forces her hands to her lap. "I mean . . . it's in the early stages. But she let me use it anyway."

"Use it . . . how?"

"I searched for Spring House."

"And that's how you found these slave narratives?"

"Yeah. They weren't all in one place until a few months ago. This project has assembled old documents that were scattered in archives all over the world."

"OK. And these slaves . . . what did they say?"

"They said the earth took Spring House," Nova answers. "The *justice* of the earth."

"Those were their words? The justice of the earth?"

She nods. "And they all mentioned one name. Virginie Lacroix." The French pronunciation—*ver-jun-ee*—rolls effortlessly off her tongue.

"Was she related to Felix?"

"Nope. She was a slave. A slave who could talk to the soil."

"What, like . . . voodoo?"

"No," Nova says, with evident distaste for the cliché. "There's no mention of Afro-Caribbean spiritual practices. No altars. No chickens getting their heads cut off. This is much more specific. She could make things *grow*. That's what they said. And apparently . . . she could also make them die."

"What?" Blake asks, incredulous.

"Seriously," Nova says. "There was a story passed among the slaves, and it was in all the accounts that came back when I did the search. They knew about Virginie's power, but the belief was that she didn't have control over it. She could use it in short bursts here and there but nothing that could have freed her or caused an uprising. Anyway, Delachaise was a terrible manager. A lot of the plantation owners were. Spoiled little French brats who weren't prepared for how labor-intensive cane harvesting was going to be. There wasn't much turnaround time each year before the winter frosts came, and there was also the refinement process and all that. Anyway, to make up for how overwhelmed he was, Felix worked his slaves half to death. So Virginie showed him what she was capable of."

"And . . . what? Killed him?"

"No, once he found her out, they made a deal. He asked her to make the cane grow faster. In exchange he'd add enough new slaves to lessen everyone's workload. In other words, he promised to stop working everyone half to death if she'd use her magic on his fields."

"Did she agree?"

"Sort of. Enough, at least, for her to grow the cane. But it sounds like he didn't hold up his end of the bargain. Because the whole thing didn't end well."

"Justice of the earth . . ."

"Three different narratives in the database said *something* came up and out of the earth and literally tore Spring House apart. The fire happened second. But whatever happened *first*—it was so goddamn bad, nobody cared when all the slaves took off for the swamp."

"Something Virginie *made* come up out of the earth?"

"Or something she unleashed by mistake."

Blake sits, thinking it over. Finally, still shaking his head, he says, "And we're the first people to read this?"

"No. We're just the first people not to dismiss it as the voodoo mumbo jumbo of a traumatized people."

But she's got more than words to present. The sketch she places in front of him is a pixelated scan of a crude ink drawing. The grand facade of Spring House is plainly visible in the background, but it's not quite to scale with the clump of stick-figure slaves standing in the foreground next to a giant oak tree. One of their own is lassoed to its giant trunk in a manner that wouldn't be possible in real life, given the tree's size. The overseer's whip has been caught in midair by a giant snake that's unfurled from one of the branches overhead. But it has no eyes, no flickering, cartoonish tongue. But if it's not a snake, then it has to be . . .

Blake knows this is the part where he should continue shaking his head in disbelief, dismissing the story as the childish folklore of a primitive and uneducated people. But he can no longer muster such a reaction, and so he sees Nova softening before him as she realizes she won't have to mount a stronger defense of this incredible tale.

"So . . . ," Nova finally says. "What did Jane Percival say?"

Blake knows his next words will amount to a kind of surrender, that much of what other people have regarded as his defining courage sprang from his belief that he had survived one of the worst blows life could deliver. But now, suddenly, the rules about what life can hurl at you have been suspended, and he hesitates, scared of what this could unleash. He knows, though, something has already been unleashed—both in 1850, and now it's happening again for some reason—and if he stays silent, it will amount to a betrayal, of Nova and her father, whose lifework is Spring House and everything that rises from its soil.

"She said the vines are coming for us all."

The eighteen-wheelers lumbering past outside seem hollow and insubstantial, their great tires skating across a line between air and earth that seems perilously in doubt. The waitress comes to refill their water glasses, but something about the tense energy coursing between the two of them causes her to recoil wordlessly, retreating behind the counter and shooting a hasty glance in their direction, as if she has mistaken the stunned silence between them for the calculation of armed robbers preparing to strike.

Then Nova's cell phone rings, and she is digging in her backpack for it, and she's *uh-huh*ing her way through what sound like pleasantries on the other end, and Blake is wondering if, just as the revelation that Santa Claus was a myth killed the Tooth Fairy, the Easter Bunny, and a host of other childhood fantasies for him, this current revelation and its spreading, unavoidable implications are opening a doorway that will admit more than one impossible guest.

Then Nova shoots to her feet and cries, "What do you mean he went *back* there?"

19

The gas station is an island of light beside the two-lane blacktop. Caitlin turns into it at the last possible second, even though her BMW X5 has over half a tank, more than enough to get her to Spring House and back to New Orleans.

The attendant looks up from his magazine behind bulletproof glass, face shaded from the sodium-vapor lights by the bill of his John Deere baseball cap. When she goes to put her credit card into the reader, she sees that there isn't one and is reminded that she's not in Uptown, but several miles up the west bank of the river from Luling, where the population is sparse and one fuel-and-run could take away half a day's business.

"Pay first," comes the attendant's voice through the speaker overhead.

Instead, Caitlin stands next to her shiny black SUV, the gas pump frozen in one hand. She figures she has only minutes left, so she opens the gas tank anyway and begins unscrewing the cap.

"Pay first, ma'am."

Just then, the sedan that's been following her for a half hour blows past the gas station. It's hard to keep track of its continued speed in the darkness, but a few moments later she sees the sedan's brake lights flash on, angry red eyes trailing away around the bend in the highway up ahead. Slowing. Calculating. Waiting?

"Pay f—"

"Fuck off!" Caitlin roars. She's staring at the attendant before she realizes she's whirled on him. The undeniable astonishment in his expression at such full-voiced fury coming from so delicate a woman chases away any remorse she might feel over her outburst, replacing it with bone-deep satisfaction.

When she nods and smiles, the guy begins reaching for something under his desk, without taking his glazed eyes off her. Whether it's a gun or an alarm button, she's not sure. And now that she's confirmed she's still being followed, there's no need for her to linger.

Fifteen minutes later she is traveling up River Road when the sedan's headlights appear in her rearview mirror again.

20

"I'm not getting this," Kyle Austin says.

"Spring House, her plantation," Mike says. "That's where she's headed." Kyle is still sitting at Scott's desk, watching the green-flared quadrants on the computer screen that show various angles on Caitlin Chaisson's now-empty house.

Mike's voice sounds tinny through the prepaid cell phone. Scott has given up trying to overhear, and now he's headfirst in the kitchen pantry, probably getting ready to stress eat or make some kind of protein shake with five shots of bull adrenaline and a meth-amphetamine chaser.

"I mean, I don't understand why you're following her. The house on St. Charles is just sitting there, empty. Shouldn't we make a play?"

"A play?"

"For the *tape*."

"Yeah . . . but this might be more interesting."

"*Interesting*. We're going for interesting now. What does—"

"Don't be such a little bitch, Austin. She's on the move, *alone*, at one in the morning—"

"So what, man?"

"So rather than looking for a needle in a goddamn *mansion*, I could maybe see if she's covering up something about her fucking husband that we could use to get the tape out of her. You get me?"

"We're not detectives."

"We're not murderers either, but that's what everyone will think if she ever wants them to."

We're not? Kyle thinks.

Across the apartment, Scott seems to have produced his own answer to the question needling Kyle's brain. He hasn't been rooting around in the pantry for protein powder or energy drinks. Instead, he's set a giant gun case on the counter from which he has removed maybe the largest handgun Kyle has ever laid eyes on. It's a 500 Smith & Wesson Magnum, so long it looks like it would be impossible to aim with one hand. Kyle's seen videos of the things online blowing the shit out of cinderblocks with a single bullet. *Handgun hunting,* they call it.

Scott's got a cocky half smile on his face until he sees the expression on Kyle's.

"Story of my fucking life," Mike growls. "Tell you what, how 'bout you kids just sit back and I'll clean up the whole mess, and when I'm done I'll bring you a pretty hat you can wear to church with the other ladies."

Mike Simmons hangs up on him before he can answer, and then it's just Kyle, Scott, and the cartoonishly large gun sitting on the kitchen counter like a prop from a comic book. And Kyle Austin thinks, *Maybe you* should *be the one cleaning up the mess. You're the one who whacked Fuller with the goddamn pipe.*

Scott's expression is suddenly pale and distant, and for a second Kyle is afraid he's about to be punished with an ass-whipping for not being visibly excited about Scott's insanely large firearm. But Scott is staring past Kyle, at the computer screen and its night-vision views of Caitlin Chaisson's mansion. And then Scott is walking slowly across the apartment, and when Kyle sees the giant handgun left all by itself on the kitchen counter, he has a mad urge to dash for it, as if it might be snatched up and wielded against them by a mentally imbalanced ghost.

"What the . . . ?" Scott finally whispers. And Kyle is forced to turn his attention away from the abandoned gun to the computer screen.

What he sees there at first appears to be a trick of shadows until he realizes there's only one concrete, physical explanation. One glass wall of the second-floor solarium is either gone or mostly shattered. He can't see the broken glass, but he can see the clouds of insects now swirling freely through the solarium's interior like a compact tornado. The cloud looks three times larger than he first thought. It looks like the bugs have knocked over some sort of appliance that's now short-circuiting. The whole scene looks like a miniature version of a transformer gearing up to blow in a violent thunderstorm. In the split second before each pulse of light overpowers the night-vision lens with sickening intensity, Kyle glimpses a density of insects to rival the clouds of Formosan termites that used to shut down Zephyrs baseball games when he was a kid.

"Did they—did those bugs . . . ?"

"Yeah," Kyle says. "I think they broke the goddamn window."

The next flash is fierce, far larger than the ones before, so bright Scott leaps back from the computer screen, one arm going up to shield his eyes. But Kyle can't force himself to look away, because there was a shape to this explosion of light that the other pulses lacked, a brilliant, brief silhouette of a form that looked halfway human as it made its way through the tumbles of hovering insects like a propulsion of fierce white dye.

But the image is so brief Kyle is able to dismiss it as a trick of the eye. What he can't dismiss is the gaping, jagged hole in the solarium's glass wall that the flash illuminated in full for the first time. And now the clouds of insects are streaming through it and taking to the night sky, so many of them it looks as if they weren't just filling up the solarium but the entire house.

21

There was a brief period in the more recent history of Spring House when Caitlin's mother entertained the idea that she would do some of its gardening herself, and the tools she purchased for this endeavor—and even used on perhaps two or three different occasions—are still in a gleaming red box inside the gardening shed, right where she left them years before.

Caitlin carries the box, along with a flashlight—the biggest and brightest she can find—to the gazebo, taking the long route through the middle of the gardens so as to give her pursuer time to catch up. She doubts she will hear his car approach, although he (she assumes it's a he) doesn't strike her as the most professional of night stalkers, as evidenced by his own arrogant over-the-shoulder wave to his own planted camera. Still, she has one goal and one goal only. To get him to visit the gazebo. Alone.

She sinks to her knees and runs her hands across the floorboards. They are cracked and jostled in places, but the damage isn't as severe as she had thought. It seems as if the vines didn't punch through them like a fist but instead somehow managed to flatten themselves in between the cracks, as snakes and rats do when they're trying to fit inside walls.

They won't need to do that this time.

She grabs a small gardening shovel and wedges its sharp tip into one of the thin cracks. After a couple seconds of prying, she's pulled free a half-foot section of floorboard. She recoils instinctively, half expecting to uncover a swirling portal to the spirit world. What lies below, however, is glistening and densely coiled and appears to be very much of this earth. These growths appear fetal when compared to the vines that nursed from her wrist; they lack blossoms and leaves, and their general shape and enmeshed pattern remind her of old illustrated versions of *Jack and the Beanstalk*.

She spends the next twenty minutes removing as many floorboards as have been jostled loose by the previous night's eruption. She tries, with each move, to strike a balance between the speed of a furtive late-night burial and the time her pursuer might need to catch up with her. It isn't critical that he see her every move, just the final act, which includes removing several magazines she found in her trunk—now wrapped inside an old T-shirt—and placing them down under the floorboards of the gazebo as if they were an item of great and secret import.

She has set the bundle atop the coiled vines and is about to retreat altogether, when she realizes her next few moves might require a little test. She runs three fingers down the side of one of the slick vines. It reacts to her touch with a leisurely, serpentine slide that makes a moist, fleshy sound.

Still connected, she thinks. *Still . . . mine?*

There's only one way to be sure.

She takes the shiny, barely used pruning shears from the toolbox and presses its handle until the blades open wide enough for her to drag one sharp edge across her left palm. The resulting wound doesn't bleed as much as her wound the night before, but it's enough. The first fat red droplets to hit the vine below are absorbed immediately, soundlessly, like water evaporating in a time-lapsed film. And then, as Caitlin holds her dripping palm out over the small shadowed cavern, the tip of one vine is lifting up into the air like a charmed cobra, and this time, because she is present and fully conscious, a delirious laughter overtakes her as she watches it twine gently around her bleeding palm, covering the wound, drinking from her silently and without effort. Her breasts are smashed against the gazebo's floor, her hair draping her face, several locks of it blinding her right eye, but she fears any adjustment will disrupt this magical marriage of earth and blood.

When it is done, it is done. It untwines from her hand, and once again a flowing wound has been miraculously reduced to a vague rosy scar; this vine has the power both to drink and to heal, it seems. And then it is drifting back down to its former resting place. The night before, it took off in immediate pursuit of her husband, the man whose terrible betrayal was freshly seared into her soul, but now it lies motionless. Waiting? If so, then for what? Perhaps because her pursuer is not yet within her immediate vicinity. Maybe as soon as he gets close, as close as Troy and his little whore were to her the night before as they hurried off to the gardening shed . . .

She replaces the floorboards as carefully as she can, taking care to leave one conspicuously loose. She turns on the gazebo's single lightbulb before heading back to the main house.

As she circulates through the mansion's silent hallways—killing the lights, pausing to undress in front of the bedroom window, giving the appearance that she is retiring for the night—the gun is either in her right hand or within reach the entire time.

Once Spring House is in darkness, she stands in one corner of the master bedroom window, the four-poster canopied bed throwing a monstrous shadow on the wall beside her. She waits, listening to familiar ticking sounds of a great house cooling in the late hours of a night in the Deep South.

When her new friend appears, a low, lumbering shadow moving through the gardens toward the gazebo, Caitlin has to stifle a laugh. It's as satisfying a moment as the gas station attendant's terrified expression. Still, she gains control, reminds herself that she has work to do.

She grips the edge of the window frame, gazes down upon her intruder as he moves toward the gazebo, and tries to summon the same hatred, the same rage she felt when she watched her husband and his little slut rushing through the same garden.

The problem, though, is that the hate is nothing like she felt (*feels*) when she thinks about Troy and Jane. *What has this man done to you? Really? I mean, except hop your fence and plant cameras in your yard? Does he really deserve the same fate as Troy?*

These thoughts, and the cold fingers of regret they press against her strained heart, have distracted her from the silence outside. Indeed, she can only hear her own rasping breaths. No screams from the gazebo, and the guy's still down on his knees, mimicking her earlier pose almost exactly, pulling up loose floorboards. The vines that slithered at just the hint of her touch, the vines she just fed for a second time, have not responded to her mental command.

She feels instantly, violently humbled, and is shocked to feel a hot sheen of tears in her eyes. But then a part of her leans into this feeling. She was moving too quickly. That's it. She doesn't even know who this man is, and she was so desperate to test the new powers available to her that she rushed into this with too much thoughtless hunger.

Magazines, she realizes suddenly, the word exploding in her mind like a bright flare. *He'll know it's a trap now. I couldn't think of anything better than magazines. And why should I have? I thought he'd be dead by now. Why isn't it working? What's different from last time?* This new question reminds her of the one that glued her to the windowsill a few moments before: *What has this man done to you?*

And as she turns that question over in her head, she can feel it shift just a bit, the emphasis changing. *What has this man done to you?*

A voice that sounds surprisingly like her dead husband's answers.

Not enough, sweetheart. Apparently not enough.

In a few seconds, her strange hooded intruder will realize he walked into a trap. He will know that he is alone with a frail young woman who has been playing tricks with his mind. Vines or no vines, Caitlin cannot have this, cannot be thought of as weak any longer, and so now she is running—out of the room, down the stairs, and through the front door—gun raised in one hand as if it has the power to part the shadows before her.

She creeps up on him silently. "Take it off!"

The guy doesn't move. He's found something down in the vines, and for a delirious instant she thinks one of them has snagged him, but he isn't struggling, he's digging. The magazines she laid as a trap have been tossed aside onto the floorboards next to him. "Stop!" she yells again, and this time his hands go up, while he stands straight and backs up at the same time.

"Stop moving and take off the hood."

Gone are the hot tears of embarrassment. She is proud of the authoritative tone of her voice, at least, if not the wobbly aim with which she holds the tiny pistol on her intruder's back.

But he's still backing up.

"I said *stop* mo—"

He spins and lunges at her in the same instant, his arms out. She sees the glint of something in his right hand and before she can process whether or not it's a weapon, she fires, and in the muzzle flash she watches her husband's blood-encrusted gold watch tumble from the intruder's hand and fall to the earth at her feet.

Just like the man she has shot.

22

"He's not here, Nova." It's the fifth time Blake has said it, but Nova keeps searching the little house as if her father might be cowering in the few inches between the wall and the back of the sofa or curled up inside the tiny kitchen pantry.

"Maybe he's been and gone?" Blake offers.

But Nova just shakes her head and keeps up her futile search, and Blake is sure she isn't as frightened for her father's well-being as she is furious he broke his promise. *Which might be the reason he's not answering his phone,* he thinks. After their conversation a few hours before and the events of the past twenty-four hours, everything seems possible, none of it good. Willie ignoring his daughter's wrath is the best of the scenarios Blake can conjure.

On their way in, they bypassed the plantation house and its grounds, taking instead the gravel road right to Willie's miniature house. Which means it's not the only place left to look.

"Nova. His truck isn't here. He's *not* here."

"Maybe he parked up at the main house?"

"Which he never does."

"No . . . but if Caitlin asked him to, he would. Come on!"

A few moments later he's running after her up the same path they took earlier that afternoon, only now the cane field belonging to the neighboring farm is a curtain of shifting shadows beside them, the sounds of its rustling stalks easily mistaken for the careful footfalls of a predator sizing up its prey.

Blake sees the gazebo first and reaches out a hand to stop Nova. The grounds are shadow-filled and so is the soaring plantation house. But the single lightbulb inside the gazebo is on, making it look like the tip of a boat dock on a dark, expansive lake. From this distance away, he can see some of the floorboards are missing, and what appear to be several magazines strewn across the dirt.

When he starts for the gazebo, Nova lets out a small sound of protest and reaches out a hand to stop him, but he takes it in his and starts leading them across the garden. She follows, silenced by his determination that they stick together. He can feel her trembling slightly through her hand.

"What the *hell?*" Nova whispers as they peer down through the gazebo's missing floor. And Blake is surprised that despite her willingness to believe, Nova is more thunderstruck by the sight of the slick and impossibly large growths coiled below than he is. Maybe it's some kind of denial mechanism, but Blake is fixated on the traces of recent human behavior all around them: the deliberately removed floorboards, the discarded red toolbox, the swirl of some sort of gold fabric wrapped up in the vine coil.

When Blake gets down onto his knees next to the hole, Nova hisses fiercely, grabbing for his shoulder, but he brushes her hand aside and braces himself against the edge of the opening with one hand while reaching down into the miniature pit with the other. As soon as his fingertips touch the strange band of gold, he can tell it's made of fabric. The thick, slick vines barely protest as he pulls it free of their coil.

Nova goes silent, her hands rising to her mouth as Blake extracts the soaked and tattered necktie. He lifts it up toward the light overhead so they can both get a good look at it.

It feels to Blake as if the simple act of holding this discovery aloft is required to draw the implications of the scene before them into a coherent picture. The vines—if that's what they are—are too thick and large and fresh-looking to have recently been disturbed by a human burial. And why would anyone just shove this once-shiny gold necktie down into their moist lair? And could a human hand have forced it to entwine with them so efficiently?

"Was this . . . ?"

"He was wearing it last night," Nova whispers through her fingers. "Troy. He was . . . That was his . . ."

The eruption of music from the main house and Nova's scream seem to come in the same instant. The song now rattling the windows of the parlor is upbeat and cheerful, and Blake can't process the jarring transition at first. It feels like he's just rolled out of bed to find himself standing on a busy New York sidewalk. But the lyrics are familiar enough to send a spear of anxiety through his sternum.

The same Faith Hill song John Fuller would play when he called Blake late at night, when he was afraid whispering sweet nothings into the phone would be overheard by his parents, and so he let the music do the talking for him by turning the volume most of the way down and pressing the receiver's mouthpiece right up to the stereo. Only a few people on earth knew John used to do that for him; Caitlin was one of them. And she is standing on the back porch now, a shadow silhouetted by a few dim lights she's just turned on in the parlor behind her. He can't see her expression through the shadows, but it looks like she's waiting to see if they've noticed her.

"Caitlin . . . ," he calls out to her, and a few seconds later, she's moving toward them.

When she's within a few yards of the gazebo, she says, "You should go, Nova."

"Where's my dad?" Nova demands.

"Not here. Seriously. You should go."

"We ne—no. We need to talk," Nova says. But her words are shaky, and the glances she's casting between Blake and Caitlin's approaching shadow suggest that she'd like nothing more than to take off running. "We need to talk about what's going on here. I'm not letting my daddy come back here, unless I *know* what—"

"I know you hate me, Nova. I know you always have. I know it never seemed like enough, the things I did for your father. For your family—"

"For *us*?" she asks, angry at the insinuation. "What the hell are you—*where is my father?*"

"—but trust me. I'm trying to protect you here. I am. Truly."

"There's nothing you *can* protect me from, *Miss* Caitlin."

"Really? Want me to tell you what we did to those three boys who cornered you that day you were walking home from school? The ones that touched you even after you begged them to stop?"

Nova is visibly stunned, lips hanging open like a grouper's as she seems to mentally reach for the memory while recoiling from it in the same instant.

"Sure, you're a big girl now with a lot of opinions and college professors filling your head with all kinds of fantasies about how things are. About how they should be. But it wasn't your father who walked those boys to the parish line and told them what would happen to them if they ever came back to Montrose Parish. It was *mine*. And he had friends with cop cars. So believe me when I tell you my family's done more for you than you'll ever know. And believe me when I tell you it's time for you to leave."

"What about me?" Blake asks, taking a few steps forward, hoping to see the expression on Caitlin's face. No such luck. But he *can* see the outline of the pistol she's holding in her right hand. "Why do I get to stay?"

Caitlin doesn't answer, and the weight of her consideration sits over them all. Blake hears Nova's sharp intake of breath, senses the start of a diatribe. "She's got a gun, Nova," he whispers. But apparently not quietly enough, because the next thing Caitlin says is, "I've got a lot more than a gun, honey."

There's that hard edge again. What had she said to him then? *All you know is flesh and bone.* It's not just hard; it's confident, knowing, self-satisfied . . . three things Caitlin has never been in her entire life.

"Fine. Come inside," Caitlin finally says. "Both of you. Come inside and meet the man who really killed John Fuller."

23

The attendant is still stewing over the rich bitch in the BMW X5 who told him to fuck off when he hears a sound like a fantail boat coming right up the highway toward the gas station where he works. The nearest fingers of swamp are too far from his little island of harshly lit concrete for a boat to sound this close. So he just sits there, blinking at the glare outside, cursing the way it masks the highway and the surrounding night sky.

He's about to leave the register and investigate when the sound gets abruptly—and violently—louder, like a chain saw revving up. It's a buzz that reminds him of bee swarms he's seen on nature shows, but there's another undertone to it, a clicking that sounds almost like his mother's press-on nails rapping against the edge of the table.

If his mother were a giant and her nails the size of butcher knives.

When the handle of the far gas pump is ripped from its holder and slams to the concrete, he figures the whole thing is a trick of the wind. But everything else outside is ghostly-still, and a few seconds later, he can make out the swarm of insects covering the fallen gas pump as if the rusted metal handle were coated in some sort of irresistible nectar.

Within seconds, a veritable second skin of insects coats the fallen pump. They're coming so fast and furious from the darkness beyond the station's island of light that he can't actually see them. He can't tell them apart either. Are they termites, roaches, cicadas? He's had creatures of all shapes and sizes slither and dart across his outpost in the late hours of the night, but never something this immense and angry.

Then they're rising into the air in several slender fingers that seem positively elegant in comparison to the thickening mass below that gave them birth. He feels his jaw go slack and hears the magazine slap to the floor at his feet.

An impossible shape is assembling beyond the glass, but one that seems vaguely familiar. It is like the finest of pencil drawings, only each pencil stroke has its own violent and barely controlled interior chaos.

The shape is over five feet tall now. And in its details he can see the woman's skinny neck and sloping shoulders. The rest of her is a mix of suggestions, as if the bugs have latched on to lingering threads of soul and dead skin and made the best version of her they possibly can. Then the shape turns its hollow head in his direction, and he sees writhing knife slashes suggesting the woman's wide, furious eyes and her snarling mouth. And with a voice that consists of a great swelling and fragile modulation of the grinding chain saw sound coming from the entire cloud, the ghost composed of insects snarls, *"Fuck off!"*

Then, as if in response to the attendant's strangled, terrified cry, the cloud disperses, and he sees the tail end of the thick fingers as they take to the night sky beyond the gas station's lonely glare, and the ghostly impression of the girl in the BMW X5 has departed on a swarm of tiny wings.

24

The first thing Blake sees in the front parlor is Caitlin's iPhone glowing in the dock atop one of the antique end tables. The dock is connected to the stereo speakers throughout the first floor, so her phone must be the source of the Faith Hill song that's threatening to knock him into the past. There are bloody fingerprints on its screen.

Caitlin adds to them by turning the music down, and in the ensuing quiet he can hear Nova breathing next to him. The rush of blood in his ears gradually takes on the rhythm of a desperate, deafening pulse. It seems his every thought, his every breath, is now devoted to assuring himself that Caitlin has completely lost her mind and slipped into a world of self-inflicted violence and delusions.

Then he sees the overturned wing chair, the bloodstained sofa cushions in a tumble on the floor. This evidence of a recent struggle guides his attention to the fat man crumpled in a fetal position on the floor next to the flipped-up edge of the Oriental rug, the same man Caitlin is now standing over. She's also pointing a gun at his head. The man's black outfit looks like a trick-or-treater's idea of a cat burglar costume, save for the silver duct tape that binds his ankles and wrists.

Compared to the man, though, Caitlin is a mess, her hair a clawed and uneven tangle, her left cheek bleeding from scratch marks. Despite these injuries, she seems radiant with feral energy, while the man at her feet is pale and wheezing from extreme blood loss.

It doesn't matter that Blake doesn't recognize the man at first, because there is enough recognition and guilt in the man's pain-widened eyes for both of them. Just the sight of his expression alone is enough to collapse Blake's self-assurances that Caitlin's slipped into a world of utter lunacy.

Which means that this man *is* somehow connected to John's murder . . . and Blake's life for the last ten years has been nurtured by a lie.

Nova's hand comes to rest on his elbow. He's not sure if she's frightened or trying to comfort him, and it doesn't matter. He is grateful just for her touch.

"You don't remember him, do you?" Caitlin asks. And it takes Blake a second to realize the question is directed at him. Before he can manage a response, Caitlin says, "Of course you don't. The last time you saw him he was wearing a mask."

"Listen," the man wheezes. "Please . . . listen . . ."

"His name is Mike Simmons," Caitlin says. "We went to high school with him, Blake. And, boy, did he fuck up. He assumed I was in on it, you see. So after I caught him in the yard, he started making me offers. And he said too much. Way too much."

"In on it? What's happening?" Blake whispers. "Just . . . tell me what's happening."

"There's a tape, you see. A tape of this bastard and his friends leaving the scene of John's murder. Troy had it. He stole it from a security system in one of the homes along the levee that night and kept it from the homicide detectives while he framed the wrong men for the murder. Troy Mangier, our *hero*, he had it for years.

And he used it to blackmail this . . . *piece of shit* and his pals. When they heard he'd gone missing, he"—and she emphasizes who she's talking about by kicking the wounded man in the stomach—"put my house under surveillance and started following me."

Blake feels as if his gaze is shrinking to a pinpoint somewhere above the man's body and just below Caitlin's chest. He is breathing through a straw and there is a tingling weightlessness throughout his shoulders and upper back that makes him feel as if the top half of his spine has gone molten.

"This is him, Blake," Caitlin says, her voice just above a whisper. "This is the man who killed John Fuller."

"No!" The man's scream is fluid-filled and lashes his gaping mouth with spittle. *"No. No. We didn't kill anyone. I didn't know about the pumping station. We didn't know . . . the water. We didn't know the water would . . ."*

Nova lets out a stunted groan. She tightens her grip on Blake's elbow just as he begins to sink to the floor. When he lands in the chair she's steered him into at the last moment, he finds his casual, seated pose to be almost sacrilegious, and so he bends forward and places his face in his hands because it feels like it's going to fall off him, along with the rest of his skin and anything else designed to armor his soft, interior parts.

He sees Troy, the handsome uniformed officer, giving interview after interview on TV, describing the arrest of Xander Higgins and Delray Morrison in precise, professional detail. He sees the man grilling steaks on the pool deck at that condo high-rise in Pensacola where they all spent a weekend together after Troy and Caitlin first started dating, when the man's installation in their everyday lives, their lives beyond tragedy, seemed like an inevitable comfort for them all, a selfless hero assuming his rightful place. Frank Sinatra croons from the nearby stereo, and the sugar-white beach looks even more fierce and brilliant than usual beneath a sky piled high

123

with gray storm clouds that drench the watery horizon but not the shore. And Blake sits on a lounge chair, knowing it will make for a perfect memory someday, the kind you take off the shelf and write poems about when your life has stalled out, when you're lonely and older and working too hard—the music and the barbecue smoke and Troy's hair and powder-blue polo shirt dancing in the hot wind off the Gulf, the great towering clouds that from this distance are all visual drama and no real rain, and Blake feeling confident that if Caitlin could land someone so handsome and brave, then surely someday he'd find someone who'd make him feel the way John could have if he'd been allowed to live.

And the whole time, there was a tape. A tape of John's real killers that Troy had hidden somewhere. There was a tape when Troy had turned from the grill that afternoon and sung along with Old Blue Eyes as if Blake were his only audience member in the theater in his mind. There was a tape as the clouds sailed from east to west and the music soared and Caitlin called down from the balcony overhead to ask them how much longer until the steaks were done. The whole time, there had been a tape. A tape that condemned two innocent men to early deaths.

And now Blake can see how Troy could gamble for hours every weekend and never lose his apartment or his shirt. But a tape like that, how long can you use it before one of your victims cracks? So he'd gone after Caitlin years later, the wealthiest young woman he'd ever come across in his years as a lying, duplicitous bastard. Even better, she was always tethered to a best friend who was sure to see Troy as a hero, sure to help Caitlin overlook any missteps Troy might take in the first days of their courtship.

And suddenly no one seems knowable, every promise the seed of a betrayal, and Blake is making sounds into his palms that don't sound quite human as Nova grips his shoulders from behind. Because never before has the full weight of something come crashing down on him quite like this, with the force and precision of the lead pipe they struck John across the head with that night.

Blake feels a feathery sensation against his fingers and opens his eyes through tears to see Caitlin crouched on her knees before him. She's taken both of his hands in one of hers, but in the other she still holds the gun. And behind him, Nova has stiffened. She's watching their captive now that Caitlin has turned her back on the man.

"I'm sorry. I'm sorry I did it this way, but I wasn't expecting you, and I was planning to . . . Never mind that. I'm not sorry. I'm *glad* you're feeling it all at once. I'm glad that you're not shutting it out, denying it. Sometimes you can be too smart for your own good, Blake. Sometimes it's important just to feel things, even when it's rage. *Especially* when it's rage.

"You can't . . . *explain* to someone that the world is not what they think it is. They have to see it for themselves. They have to *learn* it for themselves. I mean, look at me. You came to me with all those people who said they'd seen Troy in the casinos, and I refused to believe you. And what was my reward? I walk in on him fucking some whore at my own birthday party. And what do I do? I run out to the gazebo and I grab a champagne glass and I slash my wrists and I get ready to die. But instead, something else happens. Something comes up from the earth, and it drinks from me, Blake.

"Whatever this thing is, that's what it does—it drinks from you and then it *heals* you. In every way. I'm just beginning to understand it, but I know one thing. Whatever it is, it's been waiting for the blood of the betrayed. I gave it mine and it brought me justice. It saved my life and took away my grief. And now . . . now, Blake, it's time for you to give it yours."

Blake is pulled to his feet. He's not sure by whom. Caitlin's holding the gun but it's angled on the floor, and she's pulling him toward the open door. And he's letting her. When Nova grabs for him, Caitlin swings the gun on her. "Don't worry. You can be next.

Maybe those boys did more to you than you told your daddy. We can bring them here too."

"Let go of him!"

Blake feels some form of protest bubble inside him and burst somewhere around his chest before it can become words. Caitlin shoves him gently through the open back door with one hand against his back, and he stumbles forward into the porch rail, and then they're moving through the shadows toward the brightly lit gazebo. He can hear Nova in pursuit, but he can't take his eyes off their destination. Surrounded by darkness, its floorboards cast aside, it looks like an ornate cellar door. And Caitlin is dragging him toward it by one hand. "Remember when we were kids? When we tried to become blood brother and sister? When I pricked your finger? Well, this will be just like that, Blake. Only much more special. So much more special."

He can hear himself crying now, or his best attempt to hold back the sobs. He is a rag doll in Caitlin's one-handed grip, and the gun she carries is a third presence next to him, the reason Nova is following at a distance, her eyes mostly sclera, her terror evident in her inability to stand upright and the glances she's casting back at the door and the murderer they've left bound inside.

"You can't do this!" Nova screams.

"I'm not doing anything," Caitlin snarls. "I'm giving him a choice." In her free hand, Caitlin reaches down and picks up a pair of pruning shears from the red toolbox. One blade is slick with fresh blood. *She tried,* he thinks. *She tried to use her own blood to kill him and it didn't work, so now she wants mine. Needs mine. Why? Why the rush? Why now?*

"Blake," Nova wheezes. "Don't. Please. Please don't . . ."

As if to earn his trust, Caitlin sets the gun down on the ground between them. She takes his left hand in her right, the pruning shears at the ready in her left. She has angled his back to the tiny

126

pit, as if she fears the sight of those thick, slick growths under the floorboards will frighten him out of consenting.

But it is John Fuller's fingers he feels gripping his palm, not Caitlin's. Lifeless and unresponsive as the black water rises to swallow them both.

Caitlin guides him backward. His heels strike the rise of the gazebo's first step, and he finds himself stepping up and onto it. She's pushing him even closer to the open floor, and he's allowing it. Because all he feels are his own fingers grasping at John's palms, striking and slipping, flint against a steel stone.

"Caitlin . . ." All he can manage is this frail, breathy utterance of her name, but there is something in it that strikes at her, a certain tone that pierces the veil of comforting delusions she's pulled around herself in the wake of having her world cracked in two. Maybe there was grief in it, Blake wonders, grief for John that got all tangled up and came out sounding like grief for the woman Caitlin was before she surrendered to rage and whatever power has come crawling up out of the earth around Spring House. No matter its source, the sound of it has made Caitlin go rigid with something that comes off her like fury. The open shears between them tremble with the promise of homicide.

"They're coming, Blake," she says. "There were others. He's been calling them all night. They're coming."

"Why?"

"Because I told them if they didn't, I would send the tape to every news station in the country."

"You have the tape?" Blake asks.

"What does it matter?"

Blake sees it first, and when Caitlin sees the sight register in his eyes, she turns to see Nova holding her own gun on her. Her stance seems surprisingly steady, but it could be a trick of the shadows.

"Get away from him," Nova growls.

"That's not smart, Nova. Injure me and they'll simply go for the wound. Then they'll go after *you* for betray—"

"Shut up! You have no idea what this is!" Nova shouts back. "And you have no right to force it onto someone else, not this way. Not like this."

"I'm not forcing it on anyone. Grown-ups don't blame other people for the *truth*, Nova."

"You never lived the truth your whole life, you spoiled, crazy bitch. You're nothing but privilege and lies. Something finally wakes you up after being so goddamn blind for so long, and now you think you have the right to drag someone else into your darkness? No way in hell! Get away from him. Or I will shoot you. I swear to *God*."

"Yeah. Whatever." Caitlin turns away from this blast of hatred as if it were a puff of air. "We don't have time for this, Blake."

"No," Blake says.

Maybe she expected him to whisper his refusal as if it were a shameful confession and she's startled by his bluntness, because Caitlin stares at him, the pruning shears open in her right hand. "No?" she asks. "No, you won't make a—"

"No, I won't do it. I—" Just thinking through his next words has steadied his heart, but before he can give voice to them he feels a white-hot strip of pain across his chest, and only then does he realize Caitlin has slashed him through his polo shirt from his left shoulder to his right hip. Nova screams.

And then he hears the slick sound of sudden movement behind him, and Caitlin is backing away from him, arms spread, the bloody shears in her right hand. Her expression is sympathetic, and she is shaking her head back and forth as if Blake's refusal to accept her gift is as despair-inducing as a battered wife's refusal to file a police report against her husband.

When the smell hits him, he spins, one hand flying to the dripping wound in his chest. There are four of them. They have risen from the pit, and now they stand erect, snakelike, like cobras without hoods. The obscenely large blossoms have opened and are angled at Blake. And the smell coming from them is impossible: smoke, fire—and something else. The overpowering musk of unchecked body odor, so strong and pungent it seems to come from an era without deodorant or soap or any other modern cosmetics.

Blake's eyes water, and when he opens his mouth to scream—*Shoot it, Nova. Just shoot the damn thing!*—he can taste the smell in the back of his throat, and when he blinks, he finds himself staring into darkness.

. . . They have not come. The men, Felix promised her. The extra bodies that would make the backbreaking work of this prison more bearable for them all. She has waited for the wagons to bring them, waited to hear the horse hooves pounding the front drive and the soft muffled cries of new arrivals with faces as black as her own. But even though she had given him precisely the bounty he asked for, there are no new slaves. No greater and more compassionate division of labor.

She has used her power to give them two growing seasons in one— twice the amount of cane and twice the amount of money Spring House has borne every year since its creation. But there has been no trade as Felix promised.

Before her rage can turn to despair, she waits for Spring House to sleep, then she walks barefoot from the slave quarters so as to make no noise. When she reaches the edge of the field, the vast and verdant field she grew with her own magic, she lays her hands against the nearest stalk and gives the ghosts in the soil a single command.

Die . . .

There is a crackling like that of fire, but it is the skin of the cane stalks giving way as the life is sucked from each one by the earth itself. And within seconds, they are tumbling into one another like towers built on swamp. And as they fall like shadowy, rustling dominoes, Blake can see past them to where Mike Simmons floats in a halo of fiery orange, eyes wide, gagged, and bound to a chair, his very presence beyond the field a portal between the present and the past. An invitation to unleash a similar rage as the one Virginie Lacroix released into the cane fields on which Felix Delachaise and Spring House drew all sustenance.

NO!

"No!" Blake screams.

He is staring down at the clover of leaves that have opened at the tip of a new tendril—a hand extended in greeting. Not just greeting. Invitation.

He does not give his hand in return; instead he takes a step backward, beholding the impossible being before him—its glowing blossoms and its slick green stalks—and utters the only words he can manage: "Fuck off."

When the gunfire breaks out, he assumes Nova has shot at the monstrous growths before him. But the sound comes from the wrong direction, and when he turns to look, he feels a terrible pressure against his chest—he looks down and realizes the vine has taken him despite his refusal. It's wrapped around the wound Caitlin slashed in him with punitive, angry speed.

Blake pitches forward, unsure whether he's lost his balance or if the vines themselves are dragging him into the pit. By the time he hits the bottom and other coils of vine lurch beneath his sudden weight, he realizes it doesn't matter; the vine wrapped around his chest has begun to drink.

25

Nova is vaguely aware that she's holding her hands up in the air on either side of her head as she runs in a crouch. But it isn't until she lands knees-first on the floor of the back porch that her spirit seems to crash back into her body. She spins until she's got protection from the wall behind her. Her ears are ringing from the gunfire, and when she dares a peek around the edge of the doorway, she sees no sign of Caitlin, just the brightly lit gazebo and the sea of darkness beyond.

No sound comes from the lair of the vines. If the gunfire has frightened Blake into silence, it's a good sign, a sign he isn't being torn apart or injured. But he's out there, alone. From what she saw of it, the pit isn't big enough to hide in; there's nowhere for Blake to crawl in either direction.

When the shooting started, she thought she'd fired the gun by mistake, but the muzzle flares from the far side of the garden made it clear in an instant the property had been invaded. Now, if whoever did the shooting comes forth out of the shadows, Blake will be exposed. And maybe his silence isn't a good sign at all, maybe those things ate him. Because Caitlin Chaisson has no idea what she's truly unleashed out here.

She dropped the gun. The gunfire was so loud, so fierce and sudden, it felt as if the bullets were piercing her, even though they weren't. She's never been around gunfire in her life. Has never handled a gun for longer than a few seconds when she was a little girl and her father exploded into the room in a panic and tore it from her hands. *If I wanted my baby to grow up around guns, I would have raised her in New Orleans!* That was her father's mantra, and now it's left her defenseless. But none of that matters. Because she just dropped Caitlin's gun like some stupid white girl in a movie she and her friends would jeer at from the third row.

But she can see it. It lies a few feet from the back steps. From this distance, in the halo of light from the gazebo, it looks almost like a patent-leather shoe with a bright shiny buckle. And that only makes her think of the tie—Troy's necktie—they just pulled from the vines, and now Blake is down there, down there alone and silent and—

"Hey!"

Mike Simmons is draped across the doorway between the front parlor and the back porch, his wrists still bound and pressed between his chest and the floor. He's inch-wormed most of the way there on his side, and the exhaustion, pain, and exacerbated blood loss has left his jaw slack, his mouth drooling. He's the color of milk, his bloodshot eyes ringed with purple.

"Those—they're my friends," he wheezes. "She was calling them . . . threatening them. I heard her . . ."

After scanning his prone, trembling body to make sure he isn't bluffing, that he's still bound, Nova spins away from the doorway, banishes a thought about whether or not bullets could pierce the porch wall behind her, and yanks her cell phone from her pocket. She finds Blake's number.

Gun. Halfway btwn gazebo n house.

"She did this all wrong," Mike wheezes. "See . . . we can figure this out . . . She's crazy . . ."

Her phone vibrates, flooding her with relief.

Doesn't matter.

"Those are my friends," the man whines. "Please. I can talk to them and—"

"It doesn't sound like they want to talk," Nova says.

"No, no, no. *Listen—*"

"Shut up!" Nova hisses. But she can't take her eyes off the phone. *Why???*

Somewhere outside, in the great sea of darkness, a man is screaming. Mike jerks and goes still, eyes wide, drool puddling on the floor under his chin. Nova fights the urge to leap to her feet. But it's not Blake. The sound is too far away. It must be coming from the same darkness the bullets came from, the same rain of gunfire that's imprisoned her on the house's back porch, and unlike the crazed sounds Jane Percival made the night before, this frenzied, blubbering eruption carries the sounds of sheer struggle as well as agony. And now she and Mike Simmons are both silent, the victims of a terrible unwanted connection as they are reduced to audience members for this symphony of pain. This is not the sound of a fight gone wrong, or a knife wound, or a gunshot to the leg. This is the sound of someone being—she feels her lips mouth the final word—*eaten.*

Her phone vibrates in her hand with Blake's response.

Vines gone.

"Scott," Mike whispers. Fear and resistance have left his voice. He lets his head drop to the floor so hard his forehead knocks against the threshold.

She can't tell if he's crying or laughing. What's obvious is that he doesn't feel the sudden, violent shift of the floorboards beneath them, doesn't hear the rattle that courses through the wall behind her in response. Or he just chooses to ignore these things, just keeps his head pressed to the floor because his wrists are bound and there's no way to cover his eyes with his hands like a frightened little boy.

Then he retches like a cat trying to cough up a hairball, and suddenly he is rising up and off the floor.

His wrists, still taped and bound, peel out from his bloody chest and dangle in the air below him as he is righted and lifted at the same time. For a moment or two, it looks like he is levitating. But by the time his bound ankles rise several inches into the air, he is hovering at a right angle to the floor, and through the blood covering his sternum, Nova can finally make out the slick, dark tentacle that has torn through the man's stomach, then laced itself back through a hole in his throat, venting the breath from his screams.

Behind his head, a great blossom unfurls. It is a giant, cartoonish version of the flower Nova glimpsed in the spot where Troy Mangier's body should have been. The massive petals contain the fierce luminescence of another world as they open to swallow Mike Simmons's head.

26

When Blake hears footsteps running in the direction of the gazebo, he is sure he's waited too long, that he should have sprung from his hiding place and made a leap for the gun as soon as the terrible screams stopped. But he was too dazed by the sudden, silent departure of the vines that held him prisoner only seconds before, the way they branched off in two different directions, separating from each other cleanly, without the tearing of skin or the snapping of stalks, moving soundlessly into the soil, leaving him with the undeniable impression that the energy animating this life-form didn't obey the physical laws of this world as much as it indulged them.

Still flat on his back in what is now an empty, muddy hole in the earth, Blake reaches up with one hand to grab the nearest loose board he can reach without revealing himself. He draws it to his chest in both hands. Only then does he realize the long gash across his chest has healed almost entirely from the vine's patient suckling. Inside the tear in his polo shirt is a vague rosy scar that looks months old.

The footsteps crunch past the gazebo in the direction of the house, past the spot where Nova dropped the gun. Blake leaps to his feet, board raised like a baseball bat, and sees the silhouette of a man racing toward the house's kitchen door. There is nothing tensed or predatory about the man's pose as he runs. It's too dark to see if he's armed, but he doesn't hold his arms in front of him as if he's aiming a gun. He's just running like hell.

Blake sees the gun right where Nova said it would be. By the time he has it in hand, the man has disappeared into the house.

I'm not chasing him . . . yet. But something is.

Inside the grand and deeply shadowed house, he hears thundering footsteps on the staircase, someone so desperate to get distance between himself and the ground he doesn't care who hears his noisy ascent. The footsteps get louder when he hits the second floor. Doors are being thrown open. *He's trying to get higher . . . The widow's walk.*

By the time Blake reaches the second-floor landing, the man is racing up the short wooden staircase to the small platform atop the house's roof, the door swinging open behind him. Blake tears through it, taking the steps at an angle so he can keep his balance without lowering the gun.

And then, in an instant, he's reached the top, and now it's just him and the crazed, mud-smeared stranger under a star-filled sky. The roof feels like a raft floating on a sea of oak trees. Beyond the canopy of huge branches covering the front drive, River Road is a ribbon of black hugging the base of the earthen levee yards away, and just beyond the levee's dark swell, the blazing lights of a containership glide by on the river.

The man spins in place, gasping. Blake wouldn't be surprised if he waved his arms at the ship for help. But instead he searches the roof, which slopes gently away from them on all sides. There is no angle from which he does not fear an attack; Blake and Blake's new gun appear to be the least of his concerns.

He looks vaguely familiar, this wheezing, terrified stranger, much in the same way Mike Simmons was. Blake sees football team photos hanging on the walls of his high school. Rows of little faux gladiators down on one knee, clad in brilliant-white practice jerseys and pretentious scowls. They have been close before, he and this man, Blake is sure of it. Within inches of each other, in fact, during an encounter in the dark on another, more distant levee, this one on the shore of a massive lake, a spot where the prayers and intimate whispers of two frightened but very much in love young men named Blake and John lingered.

"Are you doing this to us?" the man rasps.

Blake doesn't answer.

"Can they . . . can they get me up here?"

"I don't know," Blake says, because it's the truth. "Kyle . . . Your name's Kyle Austin. You broke your leg outside the cafeteria during lunch. You and your friends had a skateboard, and you were goofing off before the teacher caught you, and you . . ." What Blake wants to say is that when Kyle rolled over all those years ago, leg twisted at an impossible angle, he wore the same contorted, agonized expression he wears now. But Blake doesn't want it to sound like he's just now remembering who Kyle is. He wants Kyle to believe this was planned. He wants Kyle to feel trapped, because people who are trapped are more likely to talk. Just like Mike Simmons started talking to Caitlin after she shot him.

"What happened down there?"

"Scott went off . . ." As Kyle slows himself to catch the breath needed to explain, the sobs start: hiccuping, pathetic. "We were supposed to meet . . . She called, said she had Mike. . . . said she wanted to make a deal, but if we didn't come tonight, she'd show everyone the tape—"

"What's on the tape?"

"Us. It's a side-street view, close to the levee. It's got us parking, putting the hoods on. Then it's got us running for it after we—after . . . Can they get up here? Those things. Can they get up . . ."

"I know how to use this gun, Kyle. I learned after what you guys did to me. Keep talking or I'll put a bullet in your kneecap."

Kyle lets out a strangled half laugh, half sob. "We came through the back way to surprise her, but when Scott saw you, he freaked. He thought she was giving you the tape and the whole thing was a setup and we'd walked into a trap . . ."

"You did."

As if a nest of wasps has been kicked over inside his skull, Kyle bends at the waist and brings his fists to his temples and screams, *"What are those things?"*

Blake doesn't answer. He doesn't say, *I don't know.* Doesn't say, *I just know how they move, and what they like to drink.*

Instead he just asks, "Why?" Blake raises his voice to be heard over a fresh round of pathetic sobs. "Why did you kill him?"

"We didn't! We weren't—we were just supposed to scare you guys. He knew you guys met there, and he thought if we roughed you up a little bit that you'd stop . . . He was our coach, I mean. We just thought . . . But we all knew Simmons was crazy about gay shit. Coach must've thought that made him right for the job, but I thought it made him wrong. Dead fucking wrong! But I didn't say anything. I should have *said*—"

"Coach?"

"Coach Fuller. But he didn't ask for a pipe. He didn't ask for a *fucking pipe* for God's sake. Simmons is on that fucking tape, stepping out of the car and swinging the thing around like he's some goddamn Viking. And nobody . . . nobody wanted . . ."

Vernon Fuller.

Blake sees the SUV parked across from the entrance to the emergency room where he works, sees the taillights as it speeds off in the milky predawn light, and now he realizes Vernon Fuller is making a last-minute escape from the living evidence of his crime. He sees Vernon Fuller, reeking of bourbon, turning in on himself in the pew at his own son's funeral, quitting his job as athletic director, leaving their school's winning football team without a coach, then divorcing his wife shortly thereafter, not even showing up at the hospital or her funeral after she got sick with cancer a decade later. Not grief-stricken. Guilt-ridden. Shattered.

Responsible.

"It's not fair . . . ," Kyle wheezes.

"Fair?" Blake asks him.

"He should be here too."

When the floorboards creak behind him, Blake spins his head, without turning his back on Kyle. Caitlin has mounted the steps to the widow's walk, her hair hastily pushed back from her forehead, but more clotted with dirt and blood than before.

"Why?" Blake asks.

"I told you. He wanted us to scare—"

"No—Vernon. Was Troy blackmailing Vernon too?"

"I don't—"

The sound that comes next is like several tennis balls spitting from a practice machine, and suddenly Kyle Austin's chin is gone, the rest of his final sentence lost in a fluid-sounding cough. The right side of his face is suddenly and hopelessly distorted by an eruption just beneath the skin, and for an instant Blake thinks the guy is about to do some clownish impression of someone and that's why his face is all messed up. But then the three glistening stalks, each the thickness of a man's arm, tug on Kyle's frozen, erect body from where they have speared it in three different places. Kyle crashes through the section of floor the vines weakened when they punched through it only seconds before and disappears in a rain of debris.

"Bye, Kyle," Caitlin whispers.

Blake watches the process repeat itself, watches Kyle hit the floor of the guest bedroom below, watches it give in exactly the same way. Kyle's limbs don't flail or tumble, but instead the vines hold him like a speared fish as they descend, wood and debris falling after him, and Kyle Austin's fatal plummet looks like the sudden flight of a jet-pack-propelled superhero played in satirical reverse.

As Blake stumbles past her toward the steps, Caitlin reaches out for him. He bats her hand away, manages to catch the banister in his free hand before he falls forward over his own feet. The back of his throat is on fire.

He rights himself and makes it to the guest bathroom before emptying his stomach into the toilet. Even as he vomits, he is aware that he's still holding the gun in one hand, that he's laid it across the back of the toilet bowl, barrel aimed at the wall. He can't let go of it even as his entire body, right down to the marrow in his bones, tries to repel what he's just witnessed. To expunge it like a virus or an infection. And he wonders if he has a space in his brain or in his soul for monsters and demons, or if he will, like most people, choose insanity when confronted with a fearsome reality.

When Caitlin begins stroking the back of his head, his body rebels against that too. In an instant, he's on his feet, gun raised, standing in the open bathroom door, and Caitlin has backed up into the hallway, shaking her head in disappointment, her hands going up.

"I said no," Blake whispers. "You asked me what I wanted and I said no."

Now there is anger in her eyes, a flash of it as she meets his stare head-on, as if he has left her alone with this nightmare simply by pointing out what she's done to him. As if he was the one who betrayed her. As if he was the one who slashed her chest and threw her into that pit. It might have been his blood that sparked the vines, but their blood was on her hands.

And the earth knew that too.

Caitlin begins to speak. Before she can get a word out, there is a terrible buzzing sound from outside, made louder by the open door to the widow's walk behind her. And from her startled expression and the way she looks dumbly to the ceiling overhead, Blake realizes this is not part of her plan, that this sound is unfamiliar to her as well. And for the first time that night, she looks frightened. When her eyes meet his, she is Caitlin again, unsteady, and full of insecurity that too often coalesces into self-hatred.

"Blake . . ."

The shadows of shifting tree branches along the sloping wall of the staircase behind her darken suddenly. Blake lets out a small cry, and Caitlin jerks at the sound, and her stare is suddenly expectant and desperate.

And then they hit her. It's a column so thick the staircase behind her goes black. The open door disappears as she's slammed into the opposite wall face-first. They're piling up behind her, like ripples in water, and there's no doubt that she is the locus, their target, that the great deafening and blinding cloud of insects now filling the upstairs hallway has come for Caitlin Chaisson and no one else. Not a single one has landed on his skin. Not a single angry thread of them heads in his direction as he backs up, the gun still raised stupidly on a target that has turned swirling and amorphous.

When Caitlin screams his name again, it's as if the bugs themselves are absorbing her voice, amplifying it while also filling it with a great and inhuman rattle. And when she peels herself off the wall, arms batting wildly at the air all around her, Blake sees that she is literally losing her very matter to them, that as they pull free from her skin, mirroring her every action now at various distances from her body, they take more and more of her with them. There is no blood, no tearing of flesh. But they *are* consuming her. As she stumbles wildly toward the top of the grand staircase, they are *devouring* her.

"*Blaaaaaaaaaaaake!*"

There is almost none of Caitlin Chaisson left in the scream. It is, rather, the voice of this terrible, all-consuming cloud of insects so tightly joined to one another it's impossible to tell what species they're composed of. And they are transforming Caitlin into something that is more writhing, desperate spirit than person, while ignoring Blake altogether. He literally does not exist for them.

At the top of the grand staircase, what remains of Caitlin inside the cloud loses its footing and goes over, and the swarm adjusts perfectly as Caitlin's vaporous remnants tumble down the stairs, losing skin and flesh and bone on their descent so that halfway down the stairs, the matter inside of the swarm looks more like an abstract, animated sketch of Caitlin Chaisson's fall than an actual person somersaulting down unforgiving wooden stairs.

At the bottom step, all traces of Caitlin the human are gone. It is only at that moment that the swarm lifts into the air, organizing itself beneath the swinging chandelier. A sudden, dizzying uniformity sweeps through each tiny member, and now there is a clicking and clattering of pincers and thicker, heavier wings. Each place within the miniature cyclone of insects Blake directs his attention, he sees bigger and more formidable creatures, flashes of stingers and antennae. But they're all moving so fast, it's impossible for him to get a detailed picture of a single one—they seem to exist only as a whole. Their buzzing sound has deepened from an outboard's high-pitched whine to something that sounds more like a motorcycle's growl.

Blake is about to fire at them. Maybe they'll come after him, but he doubts it after the way they've been ignoring him. At the very least, it will disperse them. At the very least, it will give him *something* to do other than stand there, dumbfounded, emptied of recourse or any frame of reference for what he's seeing, the gun in his hand now as powerful and protective as a fingernail clipper.

And then they're gone.

It takes Blake a few seconds to see where they've gone to, and the effort requires him to stumble halfway down the grand staircase until he can see the hole that Kyle Austin's body—*not Kyle, the vines; the* vines *broke that hole*—punched through the ceiling of the first floor. The more organized swarm of newly enlarged, otherworldly insects has spirited away up through the opening in the widow's walk floor.

His vision blurs and blackens around the edges at the same time. He hears the gun falling barrel over butt down the stairs, feels a vague distant sense of alarm that it might fire, but it doesn't. It lands at the bottom with a hollow-sounding thud. Hollow and useless against these new terrors of the night.

27

Left foot, right foot, breathe. Left foot, right foot, breathe.

It's a mantra one of the senior nurses taught him after he first started working in the ER. She'd assured him it would come in handy after the first serious trauma case was wheeled in, an accident victim so hopelessly mangled her appearance in the emergency room was more of a grim formality than a first step toward recovery.

Left foot, right foot, breathe. Left foot, right foot, breathe.

There was a trick to the little saying he learned only later. It was meant to distract you from how shallow and stunted your breathing was by giving it the weight and duration of a single footfall. A normal breath should take two steps, not one. But by saying all three of them in rapid sequence, by giving them all the same illusory value and duration, you tricked yourself into believing you weren't edging on a state of shock. And so that's what Blake Henderson is doing now.

Nova is in the kitchen washing her hands at the sink, and for a second it's possible to believe that she has somehow missed the whole thing. That she was watching television in the other room as some otherworldly force tore through the floor of the house, devouring flesh and bone, then retreating before a cloud of furious insects collected and absorbed Caitlin Chaisson as if she were a cloud of smoke. But there is steam billowing from the sink that says the water is as hot as it can go, and the bottle of soap she just used is lying on the floor next to her, and as Blake approaches her slowly, he can see her chest rising and falling, her slack, her lips sputtering with each strained breath.

"Nova?" he whispers.

And she jumps at this soft, unobtrusive sound as if it were a gunshot. Suddenly her hands are beside her head as if his slight utterance is something she must physically contain, something she must beat back before it reaches her ears. "I would like a . . . I w-would like a . . . I would like a . . ." Tears are spitting from her eyes. Her tone, though, is brittle but casual, as if she were about to ask him to pour her a glass of iced tea. It's one of the worst cases of shock he's ever seen, replete with repetitive gestures, hyperventilation, and a half-formed question that can't find its latter half.

This has been a survival skill of his for as long as he can remember, to avoid full impact of a trauma by pouring himself into concern for someone else's well-being. No matter who it is: a lover, a family member, a patient. Anyone nearby. Anyone at all. And now he and Nova are stitched together as only survivors of the wretched can truly be.

"Nova . . . ," he whispers again.

She cocks her head to one side and hisses, as if he's just done something dangerous and it's too late to stop him but she can't quite bring herself to look away. Then, she's shaking her head, and the sounds are in her throat now. No words, just stunted groans that might turn into sobs if he keeps at her, keeps doing little things to draw her back into the terrible present.

"I would like a . . . I would . . ."

Like a what? he wants to ask her. *A Bible? A gun? A Valium?*

There's only one thing he has for her, so he gives it to her fully. When she feels his arms close around her, she starts to scream and her knees go to the floor and he goes with her, holding her to him as the shudders feel like they're coming from her bones, and then there's a terrible shrill clarity to her words as she screams, *"What's happening? What's happening?"*

He knows better than to answer. Instead, he adjusts his pose so that he's kneeling before her, without freeing her from his embrace. As her screams turn to sobs, he rocks her, knowing full well that he is using the deafening evidence of her hysteria and her terror to avoid his own, that he welcomes her screams because they drown out the memory and the implication of the last words he said to Caitlin before she was *taken, swarmed, eaten*—each word fires through his head like a cannon blast: *I said no. You asked me what I wanted and I said no.*

They sit like this for what feels like forever, but Blake knows that it's not nearly enough time—that there will never be *enough* time to get over what's happened here tonight. But they have to move, and she's stilled a bit, so he slowly lifts her off the floor. She doesn't resist, and without thinking, he's collected her in both arms, bride-over-the-threshold-style. He carries her out the back door and toward the small but welcoming shadow of her father's house in the distance, and it seems as if all those hours in the gym trying to armor himself against another assault by shadows has strengthened him only enough to carry a girl lost to terror across a dark and muddy expanse, beneath which an unknowable evil, freshly sated, now slumbers again.

Blake wonders if there is a lesson there, and more important, will it still be there, ready for him to wipe the dirt from it and study it more closely should this madness ever come to an end.

28

He wants to play music, but he's afraid it will drown out the approach of monsters.

He wants to hold her again, but that might upset her, and the only thing he's sure of right now is that he can't bear any more of Nova's screams. So he leaves her on the sofa in her father's tiny house while he sits on the footstool a few feet away, trying to ignore the fact that he's rocking back and forth like a senile person who only feels at home on park benches.

Nova's eyes are slitted and vacant. Her fetal pose is that of a thumb-sucking toddler, only her hands are balled against her chest and trembling. Blake fears there's a very real chance Nova Thomas might not come back from all this. It's an irony so cruel as to be vicious—she was the one who tried to convince him something terrible had awakened underneath Spring House, after all.

Blake jumps when he hears footsteps outside. Nova is still.

The screen door whines on its hinges, and a pleasant smell hits Blake. *It can't be anything as ordinary as cologne,* he thinks. It must be the cloying musk of some impossible new creature composed of flowers and insects. But then Willie is standing in the living room with them. Something about him seems different, and Blake finds himself perfectly willing to accept the man before him as a hallucination.

The smell of cologne is stronger now. The older man's chest is heaving with frightened breaths, and Blake realizes Willie Thomas looks different because he is scrubbed and coiffed and dressed to impress. A powder-blue long-sleeved dress shirt, the top few buttons undone, showing off his shaved chest, silk pants the color of café au lait. He's come from a night on the town, Blake realizes, and he looks like he's had a good time. But one glance at his daughter and he's down on one knee next to the sofa, stroking her forehead.

Nova clutches his shoulder, but this isn't enough to reassure Willie that his daughter still walks among the living and the sane. He grips her face in both hands, studies her as if the secret to her condition will be written in her sclera.

"Where were you?" Blake asks.

"She didn't answer her phone. I was callin' and callin' . . ."

"Your sister said you came here."

Willie shakes his head. "I got a lady . . . in N'Awlins . . . Nova, she don't . . . I don't like to talk about it in front of . . ." It's clear Willie isn't sure whether or not his daughter will hear these words even now. "I didn't tell my sister where I was, 'cause I didn't want her in my bidness . . . She jes thought I came back here, but I was at Dooky Chase with a lady. That's all. That's all . . ." His final words become a gentle cooing assurance his daughter can't seem to hear.

"Willie . . ."

"What happened here?"

"I—have you been to the house?"

"No. No . . . I came right here. Then I saw your cars, so I—Mister Blake, what *happened* here?"

Nova is crying silently. It's her father's voice, no doubt, and her father's gentle touch. The feel of both have pulled her back inside

148

her body, and while the return might be painful for her, Blake is relieved to see it.

"Willie, I need you to tell me everything about this place. Everything you wouldn't tell me today when we were in the shed looking at those holes."

He can see the resistance again in Willie's furrowed brow, in the long and deliberate way he looks back at his supine daughter.

"Spring House is falling apart, Willie. You don't need to carry it on your back anymore."

"What did she do?" Willie whispers.

"Nova? She didn't—nothing. She's a—"

"Miss *Caitlin*. What did she do?"

Only when his vision of Willie wobbles and splits does he realize his own eyes have filled with tears. He blinks them back, listens to his shallow breathing as if it is the gentle ticking of a clock and he's all by himself, trying to meditate.

"I ain't got no secrets 'bout dis place," Willie finally says. "It was like she said today in the shed. More of a feelin' than much else."

"A feeling?"

"Plants never act right 'round here. They *move* when you ain't lookin'."

"Those are events, not feelings."

"Maybe . . . Maybe not. But they always happen when you ain't looking, so it's not like they can be proved. But what they gave me—dat was the feelin'."

"What kind of feeling?"

"I ain't never seen no lady in a white dress floatin' over da yard or some slave draggin' her sad old behind 'round the attic singin' some kinda spiritual. But maybe . . . It makes me think, maybe ghosts, they don't act like they do in the movies. They don't jes move the dishes and the chairs when we ain't looking. They move everything and everyone. They like air and water. 'Cause they everywhere

149

is where they are. They in the ground, they in the leaves. They sideways and all through everything . . . and waitin' to be fed."

Every monstrous surge that bore down on him over the past hour—from the vines that suckled his chest to the clouds of determined insects that literally carried away Caitlin's soul—seemed possessed by a single predatory force, and Blake can think of no better description for it than the soft poetry Willie just whispered.

"Miss Caitlin . . . she fed 'em, didn't she?" Willie asks.

Blake can only nod.

"I always thought it was magic, not ghosts. The way the flowers here would move and dance. And I thought it'd be good, Mister Blake. I thought it'd be a *good* thing for her . . ."

"For who? Caitlin?"

Instead of answering, Willie cups Nova's forehead, and Blake realizes the *her* in Willie's last sentence must be his own daughter, Nova. Somehow the magic in the soil here would be good for Nova, but how?

"Caitlin . . . ," Willie says quietly, but his attention is focused on his daughter, and Blake feels like the mention of Caitlin's name is just Willie's attempt to distract him. "Where's Caitlin?"

"Gone," Nova answers, in a clear and steady voice that sounds free of both tears and shock. And then she begins to tell her father what happened.

29

In room 14 of the Hibiscus Inn, Taletha Peterson distracts herself from the dry and passionless thrusts of her latest customer by doing a mental inventory of the cars she passed on her way in. In her mind's eye, she tries to re-create the scattering of pickup trucks parked around the motel's sad, lightless swimming pool and its wilting chain-link fence. The battered Nissan Sentra, the one with the faded Save Our Lake bumper sticker, is probably her best bet if things go south. Too bad she can't remember exactly where it is.

She'd wager her stash the car belongs to Clay, the quiet, pimply kid who works the graveyard shift and always smells like bug spray no matter how much body powder he uses. Hell, maybe the body powder is what makes Clay smell like that white pickup truck that used to belch through Taletha's old neighborhood late at night, rank smoke billowing from the pipe in back, smoke that sent spiny buckmoth caterpillars tumbling to the hood of her mother's car. Or maybe Taletha's just too damn sensitive, which is what her daddy always used to say right before he'd mess with her. She's sensitive when it comes to smells, that's for sure. She prefers the men in her life to smell like nothing at all. That way they'll be easier to forget.

Clay's a nice guy. Clay lets her bring johns to empty rooms as long as she slips him a few twenties every now and then. Twenties, not fifties. And not hand jobs like most of the motel managers she works with. There was a time in Taletha's life when a man had to do more than not demand sex for favors for Taletha to consider him a nice guy, but that's a hazy period now, so far from this dingy motel room that it's a distant country. A faraway land beyond vast, deep lakes dug by a glacier named Phil, a drummer who took her for everything she was worth—which wasn't much—but not before treating her to the first suck of lung-burning, head-clearing bliss from a glass pipe.

Where the hell was that Sentra parked? Close to the front office so Clay could keep an eye on it? It's only been ten, maybe fifteen minutes since she walked past the thing, her latest customer, Mr. Lawyer Pants McUptown, hot on her heels and smelling of whiskey, and still she can't place that damn car.

If she could shut her eyes maybe, try a little astral projection, or whatever her sister used to call it. But Lawyer Pants—on his first visit, he said his name was Charles, but that was probably bullshit—is taking her missionary, and with each graceless thrust he stares down at her with the pained intensity of a man trying to take a dump.

She remembers another vehicle parked outside, one of those mini-RVs you can rent these days, the kind with the rental company's logo painted in bright, cheery letters along the side, letters that seem to scream, *Been out of my element for months! Please rape and murder me!*

But Taletha doesn't know if those things have an alarm, so the Sentra's going to have to be her fail-safe. If for some reason things go to shit inside this mildew-smelling little room with its plaid curtains and growling window-unit air conditioner, she'll run for the Sentra and kick its rear bumper hard enough to set off the alarm.

Sometimes that's all it takes. Sometimes the alarm is enough to freeze a psycho where he stands, the belt still raised over one shoulder or the gun she didn't notice aimed at her disappearing shadow, his head still swarming with sick-fuck ideas he didn't have the balls to mention when they were arranging a price. And sometimes that's not enough, sometimes a few people will have to pop out of their rooms first. And then other times, times she wants to forget, she just has to run like hell and grab for the nearest handful of rocks. But whatever the case, a car alarm in the middle of the night has saved Taletha Peterson's ass (and her face and her breasts and her fingers) on more than a few occasions.

Suddenly Lawyer Pants flips her over like she's a sack of potatoes, slides one arm under her waist, and pulls back until she's on all fours. She's afraid he's sensed how far she's slipped from her own body, from their passionless rutting, but she also needs to give him a gentle little reminder—doggy style's cool but the backdoor's off-limits. But before she can address either issue, she's distracted by a dark flutter in the lamp's frail glow. Suddenly Mr. Lawyer Pants is back inside of her—the traditional way, thank God—and Taletha is staring at the giant bug that's just landed on the man's wedding ring.

Last time the guy took care to stuff the little gold band in his jeans pocket before he stripped down. But tonight he's drunk, so he left it out on the nightstand. It looks tiny and insignificant now, but maybe that's because the bug resting on it is about the length of Taletha's index finger.

. . . *and it's staring at me.* These words shudder through her, bringing unwanted life to parts of her body she instinctively knows how to deaden before every trick. If it were any bigger, she would figure it was a Halloween toy some jerk was controlling with a string. But it's just big enough to be . . . *wrong.*

And the color, a black so deep she finds herself groping for the right word to describe the shade. It's a word that seems fancy, but she's heard it before a bunch of times throughout her life, just not to describe a damn bug. Black as night. Black as . . . lava. *Obsidian.* The color of cooled, frozen lava. Despite its size, the bug is so black its individual features are impossible to discern, except for the two forelegs that rest atop the gold band, whisking slightly back and forth as if they're kissing the metal. She's seen squirrels that are like this, so accustomed to humans they're not afraid of them. But a *bug*? This thing is *perched*, birdlike, patient, positively studious.

"What *are* you?" Taletha whispers. But she's loud enough to cause the man on top of her to jerk and go still.

"Oh, for fuck's sake," he curses.

His feet hit the carpet, and as he stumbles toward the night-stand she can't tell if he's as bothered by the bug's wrongness as she is, or if he just wants the damn thing off his precious little ring.

Taletha has pushed herself halfway across the bed by the time the man swats at the insect as if it were just a housefly. It takes to the air, its wings each filled with a glistening pattern that looks like oil floating on water. Then the bug is gone.

Taletha says, "Where did it—"

Lawyer Pants makes a sound like he's been kicked in the chest. Lightning bolts of pain seem to shoot through the man's body as he stumbles backward across the room. And Taletha is as stricken by his gape-mouthed silence as she is by his shuddering and by the tears sprouting from his eyes. The stuttering groans that rip from his chest sound like some little kid's parody of monkey sounds.

The bug is gone. Taletha can't see it anywhere.

It must be clamped between the guy's hands, which are still clasped in front of him even as his back slams to the wall.

Blood pours from between the man's fingers. His hairy legs crumple under him like windless flags. Once his ass hits the carpet, his arms go lax too—his hands unclasp and that's when Taletha sees the gaping red hole in his right palm. *He crushed it,* she thinks. *He crushed it and it stung him, and now he's dying.*

But the hole is too big for a stinger, and she didn't remember it having a stinger to begin with, and . . .

Then the bug flies toward her out of the man's open mouth.

Clay Lee's uncle has owned the Hibiscus Inn for thirty years, and because Clay is not a reader, he gets a panicky feeling in his chest when his uncle talks about the days when all the TV stations used to sign off around midnight with some recording of the national anthem, leaving whoever was stuck behind the motel's front desk with a pile of magazines and some shitty paperback novels.

Clay is relieved those days are long gone. Clay is relieved that the television people finally came to their senses and realized that there is another America out there, an America of men and women who have to spend the graveyard shift behind a desk and need round-the-clock reruns of stupid cop shows and repeats of the ten o'clock news or else an unexpected late-night customer will walk in on them playing with themselves and then they'll have to explain the whole thing to their mother and maybe get fired by their uncle.

Not Clay. On a job he can never quit unless he wants to get kicked out of his mother's house, Clay has round-the-clock entertainment, and that's why when he hears a loud crash followed by a car alarm, he assumes it's coming from the episode of *Law & Order: SVU* he's been struggling to follow for a half hour now. But the folks on the idiot box are standing inside a morgue talking over a dead body. Not a car in the shot. In fact, it's been several scenes since anyone in the episode has actually gone outside at all.

Headlights flash in the front office's glass wall, winking out a mad accompaniment to the bleating alarm. At first Clay thinks they belong to a car that's stalled out on the highway. Then he realizes they're a reflection, a reflection of his car.

The first thing he sees when he bursts from the office is the open door to room 14 clear across the parking lot, the dull glow of one of the lamps within. Then he sees one of the lounge chairs from beside the swimming pool resting inside the shattered rear window of his Sentra. Someone's thrown it so hard it's sitting half-in, half-out of his car, and that someone has to be Taletha, because she's down on all fours, back rising and heaving, the sounds coming out of her a mixture of retches and sobs. He's not sure whether to run to her or from her, and the battle between these urges freezes him in the office's door.

He's calculating the cost of the broken window and trying to recall the last time his mom nagged him to renew his insurance policy when he hears a sound louder and more grating than Taletha's wheezing. It seems to be coming from room 14, and it makes him think that the only thing worse than forking over a bunch of dough to fix his own shit car will be the amount of free overtime he'll have to give his uncle if one of the rooms gets destroyed on his watch.

He's almost past Taletha when she reaches out and grabs the leg of his pants with a clawlike grip. "Don't," she gasps. "Don't go . . . over there."

He shakes himself free, confident whatever's buzzing away inside room 14 won't be as impossible to deal with as some meth-head hooker who just wrecked his ride.

He's about ten paces from the doorway when he sees what at first he thinks is a ghost. But it's not. It's a man, a man he glimpsed only minutes earlier as he walked across the parking lot with Taletha, only now this man is standing by himself in the middle of the room, arms spread in a lazy-looking parody of a crucifixion, and it takes a few minutes for Clay to realize the man is hovering several feet above the floor. The force that seems to suspend the man is what's distracted Clay, rendering him as mute and paralyzed as a pilgrim at Lourdes. They have to be bugs, but they are blacker than any bug he has ever seen, and there is an elegance and organization to their cyclonic swirl that almost masks the horror of the scene. And in the all-encompassing grip of this swarm, the man's body is being eaten away with such speed and precision that not a single drop of blood hits the carpet below, and in another few moments, he will be gone. Ground away, rubbed out.

From within the cold, expanding prison of his shock, Clay wonders if the bones will be all that's left at the end of it. If they'll fall to the carpet in a dry tumble, and if out of respect for the man, he should wait for this awful moment.

Behind him in the parking lot, a man is screaming now. A man who's left the door to room 5 open behind him as he races for the highway. The lamp inside has been knocked to the floor during the man's escape, but Clay can see what, from this distance, appear to be tiny droplets of black circling through the entire room, a cloud just like the one inside room 14.

Still down on all fours behind his Sentra, Taletha places her palms against her open mouth, brings them away, places them against her mouth, and brings them away, and he realizes she's been doing this ever since Clay shook his leg free of her grip.

She must think they're inside of her, but Clay knows they aren't. Clay knows if they wanted her, she'd be dead already. Because these things, whatever they are, they don't fuck around and they don't feel the need to hide.

The man who burst from room 5 is standing in the middle of the highway now, waving his arms at nothing. Clay wonders if one of the swarms got him, if he's trying to wave them away, but his movements are still his own, and when a truck swerves to avoid him before slamming on the brakes, he sees the man is untouched, unharmed, just like Taletha. Just like him. And when the driver of the truck steps out, shouting obscenities, the man collapses in his arms, bawling like a baby.

Then something brushes Clay's face. He's staring at one of them. It's hovering inches from the tip of his nose, so black he could mistake it for a fragment of shadow if not for the buzz of its wings.

Taletha sees it and lets out a strangled cry. The sense that the insect is staring into him—into his *soul*—is no more preposterous than any of the other horrors he's just witnessed, and so Clay Lee feels his limbs go lax, feels a kind of surrender take him, and believes, in some fundamental and primitive way, that if he's obedient during this examination, he will make it to the other side in one piece.

And he's correct.

Whatever this creature is, it sees nothing in Clay that will satisfy its demonic hunger, and so after a minute of study it zips off into the shadows to join one of the several feasts now taking place in different rooms of the Hibiscus Inn.

And for the first time Clay starts to see the larger pattern, not just the open doors and the U-shaped layout of rooms and parked cars all around him, but a kind of awful regularity to the skin-rending impossibilities blanketing the Hibiscus Inn.

Taletha is still on her knees a few feet away from the car she just wrecked, out of her mind with fear but physically unharmed, trying to cough up a bug in her lungs Clay is sure she's just imagining. But her rich, shifty-looking john, the same asshole who always made a point of avoiding Clay's eyes when he scurried past the front office, was just turned into bug meat. And the man who just ran from room 5 and into some truck driver's arms is Sidney Dautreaux. The guy works most of the year offshore, but he occasionally spends a night at the Hibiscus Inn so he can stick it to Lisa LaPearl, whose been married to that drunk Joseph Marigny for about five years now and doesn't have the guts or the money to leave him. Clay saw Lisa and Sidney go into room 5 together after he handed Sidney the key not thirty minutes ago, but now there's no sign of Lisa at all, just another furious buzz of insects inside the room she should have come running out of, screaming bloody murder. But she didn't.

She still hasn't. She didn't run and he can't hear any screams— just more bugs.

Because they're eating her too.

But not Sidney. Not Taletha. And not him.

And that's when it hits him, a conclusion so simple it feels like a strange, sudden comfort amid the surrounding horror.

It's the cheaters, Clay Lee thinks. *Son of a bitch, they're only eating the cheaters.*

30

Blake wanted to go back to the main house alone, but Willie wouldn't let him, and there was no leaving Nova there by herself. So the three of them are walking close together through the garden's small maze of fountains and waist-high hedges when a sound comes from underneath the gazebo like mud being hurled into a wood chipper.

The gazebo's entire floor surges upward. Nova screams and throws her arms around her father. Willie raises his shotgun in a practiced grip. Silence falls. The gazebo now looks like it's tilting atop a small lava dome, several feet above ground level.

Nova's breaths sound more like whimpers. Willie makes no move to lower the oily-looking firearm. He has changed from his silk dress pants into a pair of blue jeans, and the cartridge of shells makes an obscene bulge in his front pocket.

"I thought you said it didn't care nothin' 'bout us," Willie finally says.

They've been frozen for a good five minutes, awaiting the next horrible event.

"I said it *targets*," Blake says. "That's what I said. The vines, the bugs . . . they go after specific people and they all have to be guilty of the same—"

The gazebo crackles. Willie straightens, raises the gun. But it's just a dull clatter of floorboards falling into the pit, which is now a few feet deeper thanks to the sudden pregnancy of the surrounding walls. A few seconds later, the overhead light inside shorts out, its wires severed by the eruption.

"It's a process," Blake says, once he has his breath back. "That's what I said. Whatever this thing is, it's a process . . ."

"Somebody around here feedin' blood to those vines *right now*?" Willie asks. "What's all this . . . *nonsense* got to do with the process?" He jerks the shotgun's barrel in the direction of the tilting gazebo.

"I don't know. The bugs, maybe."

"The bugs?" Willie asks. "The ones that took Caitlin?"

"Yeah, the way they left . . . it was like they were headed somewhere. Maybe whatever they're doing is causing that. I don't know. It's all connected. That's all I know. It's connected . . ."

Blake is only a few feet from the main house when he sees a crystalline pulse of light reflected in the front parlor's chandelier.

He stops in the doorway, hoping to absorb every detail of the room before he crosses the threshold.

The holes in the floor are just like the ones they saw in the shed earlier that day, only with splintered rims. The story of Mike Simmons's vain struggle against the vines is written in a long trail of drying black bloodstains that move from the varnished hardwood just inside the doorway to the Oriental rug. But here again is evidence of the vines' precision, of their ability to punch through solid objects with preternatural efficiency. These surgical details remind Blake that it was really Kyle Austin's *body* that tore gaping holes through each floor, from the widow's walk on down, not the vines themselves, and suddenly the urge to vomit returns with eye-watering vengeance.

So he focuses on the flower that emerges gracefully from a splintered hole in the middle of the floor. It's a vital, fully powered version of the one he saw in Caitlin's solarium that evening. A perfect match with Nova's description of what she saw in the shed right after Troy vanished. The pulses of bright light that flush its white petals seem to have no beginning, end, or specific center, and Blake can't discern a specific rhythm. They are not mere bioluminescence; they are a presence, a glow that looks powerful enough to float free of the plant structure itself.

He's half-afraid that he'll be hypnotized if he stares at them for too long. But that would be a charm compared to the other vicious capabilities of these plants, so he doesn't force himself to look away.

He blinks madly and wonders if the chandelier overhead is devolving into hallucination, but the bugs dappling its crystals appear solid and shaded and real. The profusion seems unholy, but the participants are everyday creatures, nothing like the winged black monsters that exploded throughout the foyer after Caitlin was consumed; these are cicadas, houseflies, and moths. And he wants to believe it's the chandelier's soft glow that's drawn them here, but he knows this is just his desperate desire to cling to the last vestiges of an ordinary world.

It's the flower they are drawn to, the same glowing, impossible blossom onto which Nova is now emptying an entire can of lighter fluid. Willie's expression suggests a collision of urges: should he lower the gun and pull his daughter back, or should he keep the firearm at the ready in case all hell breaks loose?

Over one shoulder, Nova says to Blake, "Back up! Now!"

Blake moves away as far as the doorway to the back porch. Nova pours a thin trail of lighter fluid several feet out from the blossom. The massive white petals glow unapologetically despite having been doused. She flicks off the child safety on the fireplace lighter in her left hand, brings the tiny, focused flame to the puddle of fluid at her feet.

The fluid ignites in a single, blink-fast whoosh. The flames are instantly sucked up and over the flower and into the air above.

Nova rocks back off of her knees, her butt hitting the floor with a hard thud. Willie jumps back a step.

The bugs explode from the crystals in a frenzied cloud.

The flames, which have become a single arc of blue and orange, race up the outline of some vague and previously invisible shape that fills the air above the unmarred blossoms. A hint of a face or a silhouette, Blake can't tell. But it's there for a second, and then all of it's gone, like the fire has been consumed by the air itself, and save for a scorch mark in the spot where Nova first touched the lighter to the fluid, there's no evidence of her attempt to destroy the flower at all.

All of it happens so fast Blake's attention ends up on the bugs again. A swirl of blue fire just ignited below them like a giant Bunsen burner, and it still wasn't enough to force them into full retreat. They had moved, agitated, but now they close over the chandelier again, a buzzing, swirling testimony to the draw of whatever dark power resides within the blossom's undisturbed glow.

When Blake leaves the room, Nova and Willie don't move, and he figures they're still stricken by the pale suggestion of a ghost that was briefly illuminated by Nova's unsuccessful attempt to destroy the flower.

In the ruins of the small study just off the foyer, beneath the ceiling destroyed by Kyle Austin's speared body, Blake finds the second blossom, a mirror image of the first, just as vital, just as illuminated, a slender thread of fierce beauty amid the dangling Sheetrock and overturned leather-tufted desk chair. Lining the holes in the ceiling are more regiments of hypnotized insects. They're gathering here around this blossom as well.

Blake stumbles into the house's grand foyer, because here there is no wreckage or debris or veins of june bugs and flies dappling the walls or the great chandelier. Just a tilting portrait of Felix Delachaise on the wall overhead, with his high-domed forehead and lips so fat they appear to be peeling away from his mouth, and the fresh memory of Caitlin's dismantling. As realization breaks over him, Blake reaches for the doorknob because the only thing he can think to do is run. But from behind him comes Nova's voice, as clear and decisive as a whip crack.

"You said no."

She's standing in the door of the study. Behind her, Willie stares down at the second blossom with a vacant, glaze-eyed expression.

It feels like he's breathing through a straw, but Blake manages his next words carefully, as if he were speaking to a mentally handicapped patient. "Those bugs are going to . . . I don't know . . . *react* with those flowers, and then they're going to turn into something like what—"

"You said *no*, Blake."

"I know what I said, Nova."

"Well, it has to mean something. It *has* to. She *forced* it on you. She manipulated you; she overwhelmed you. She dragged you out there, and even then, even *then*, Blake, you said no. You made a choice. That's got to mean something."

"I don't think she gives a shit," Blake whispers.

"Caitlin?"

"No. Not Caitlin."

"Then who are you—"

"Virginie. Virginie Lacroix."

They're standing a few feet apart now. Willie watches them from the doorway of the study, the shotgun leaning against the door frame in a final gesture of surrender to the powers at work all around them. In another few minutes, Felix Delachaise's portrait will probably slip from its hook and crash to the floor, and then his furrowed brow will make it seem as if he's angry at being dropped and not struggling to process what happened to Caitlin Chaisson, which is how he looks right now.

"I'm talking about the ghost of a slave who can make plants grow and die with her bare hands. I'm talking about the woman I saw when I smelled that flower. All of this, it's—it's *Virginie* . . ." He turns to the gardener. "You're right, Willie. She's sideways and all through everything and waiting to be fed. And now she has been. She got Caitlin's blood, and now she's got mine and she's going to do the same thing to me she did to her."

"You don't know that!" Nova screams, but her building hysteria tells him she believes every word that's just tumbled from his mouth in a mad rush. "You don't know what any of this means."

"I know what I can *see*. And I see a process. I see a *pattern*. And it's starting all over again. I don't know how long I have. A few hours, maybe. A day. But they're going to come for me, Nova. They're going to come for me, and they're going to . . . *take* me too."

When Nova embraces him, Blake is so startled his next words leave him. She holds to him so tightly he feels as if his bones are going to crack, as if in a fit of childish anger she's convinced she can literally armor him against the forces she knows will come for him soon. Willie has moved in a few steps closer, as if he too thinks that by closing the circle there's something they can do. He holds back, though, as if knowing that the gesture would be just that: a gesture.

"You ain't gonna run?" he asks Blake.

"Where would I go? She took one of those flowers all the way to New Orleans and those . . . things, they still came for her. Right here, they got her."

"Maybe they can't go much farther," Willie offers, voice trembling. "Maybe you could outrun 'em if you tried."

"I don't think so," Blake whispers.

"You don't *think* so?" Nova cries, pulling away from him. "What the hell does that mean? You don't *wanna* think so. Is that it?"

Willie and Nova stare at him the same way he's seen a thousand distraught relatives stare at a doomed loved one in the ER, and it's more than he can handle.

Blake hears Nova's footsteps behind him as he races through the study and then the front parlor toward the open back door. Then she falls into step with him as he stalks toward the gazebo.

"The bugs, they were normal until they got Caitlin, right?"

"I don't know, Nova. I don't—"

"You *do* know! They were normal when they came down through the widow's walk in a big cloud. They were still just bugs. They only changed after they tore her apart."

The red gardening box is still upended a few yards from where the gazebo now sits atop a baby Indian burial mound. His eyes search the grass for the pruning shears Caitlin slashed him with. Because the gazebo's light had shorted out, the lights from the main house throw Blake's and Nova's shadows across the gazebo's frame, making it look even more ruined than it actually is.

"We can get them before they get you, is what I'm saying, Blake. We can put you somewhere safe and use you like bait. Then we can blow the fuckers up. We're all from Louisiana here. We know how to kill a bunch of bugs, for Christ's sake!"

"Blow them up? Just like we burned the flower in there?"

Blake picks up the shears and tests them in one hand.

"Don't do this!" Nova shouts, and that's when Blake realizes she thinks he's about to stab himself through the heart, end his own life before a cloud of possessed insects can do it for him. But that was

166

never his plan—he knows exactly what he needs to do for the first time since getting that panicked early-morning call from Nova.

So he doesn't kill himself—he jumps into the pit instead. He's not prepared for the darkness below. It's deeper now and the bed he's landed on is softer, thicker. Overhead Willie's footsteps punch mud, and he joins his daughter's dark silhouette over the opening.

"Blake?"

At least he finally stopped calling me Mister Blake, he thinks. He's startled by the bitter laugh that rips from him. The vine he's pulled up in one hand is about as thick as his wrist. When he starts cutting, he half expects the slick tentacle to fight back, maybe try to pull his arm out of its socket. He doesn't care. He's marked for death anyway. If anything, a bad injury might force Willie or Nova to put him out of his misery, and maybe that would be better. Better than what he's planning.

But the vines don't fight back. It's too dark to see if they're bleeding in some way, but he doesn't feel any moisture on his fingers aside from their slick outer coating. The very flesh of them is parting like bread dough under the shears, just like it branched off into two different structures before traveling through the mud in pursuit of John's killers.

"Back up!" Blake shouts. As soon as Willie's and Nova's silhouettes leave the shadowy opening above, Blake tosses the three-foot section of vine he's hacked free up through the hole. Then he crawls out after it.

On his feet now, Blake picks up the piece of vine in both hands and studies it. When the beam of Nova's flashlight hits it, Blake sees what he can already feel: both ends are curling gently around his hands, like an affectionate but lazy cat seeking attention.

The flashlight blinds him when he looks up, and he's glad he can't see their faces. He doesn't want to see the man he used to be dying in their eyes.

"You ain't even gonna *try* to live?" Willie asks quietly.

"Your daughter's right, Willie. She's always been right."

"How's that?"

"This place is cursed. Get the hell away from it. Either run like hell or burn it to the ground . . . or both."

He takes off running in the direction of Willie's house before either Nova or Willie has time to process these parting words. As he runs, Nova screams his name, her voice growing hoarser by the second. But the sounds of her screams recede. She's not following him and neither is her father.

His car is still parked in front of Willie's house, and this seems like a blessing given how much the earth has moved all around him in just an hour. Once he's inside and behind the wheel, he sets the vine down on the passenger seat. By the time he's managed to pull his shirt off over his head, the vine has crawled snakelike over the gearshift, hungry for his touch once again. So Blake takes it with both hands and raises it to his bare chest. Whether it's the simple warmth of his skin or the hot pulse of his blood beneath, the vine likes what it feels. It adheres to his flesh without biting him or stinging him or in any way breaking the skin. He wonders if it's drinking from cuts too small for him to see, but nothing about its feel is similar to the terrible suckling it inflicted upon him in the pit. This is sensual and gentle, the way one end is crawling half over his shoulder, the rest of it snaking down over his abdomen. Then, careful not to disturb it, Blake slides his shirt on and tugs it down over his new, otherworldly secret with the gentle hesitation of a nervous parent swaddling a newborn.

31

Nova stares at the empty field where Blake had merged with the shadows and then vanished. The Maglite in her hand rises and falls with her long, deep breaths, causing the halo to sway across his leg like a lantern rocking in a steady wind. The silence that now blankets Spring House feels cloying, deceptive.

"Naw," Willie finally says, and it's more of a groan than an utterance. "Now where's he goin', baby? Where the *hell* is he goin'?"

For years Nova suspected her father of harboring a greater love for the Chaissons than he did for his own family, and assuring herself this love was nothing but self-loathing and a deep-rooted sense of inferiority did nothing to assuage her jealousy.

But now Nova can see that her father is a man who has tied his sense of self-worth, his very sense of security, to his ability to keep the people around him united and content. And he's just failed. For the first time she understands this controlling desire within him. She feels compassion for his desperate need to knit a community together of the nearest available candidates and wrap it around himself to stave off the terrible fear that life is just a mad riot of other people's unquenchable appetites. It took paying witness to hell on earth for Nova to get it, but she does. For the first time, she can see it.

Her father turns and meets her gaze through the soft glow cast by the flashlight she's now aiming at his waist to avoid blinding him. "I don't know . . . I don't know what to do, baby girl. I jes don't . . ."

"Oh, Daddy."

"Where's he goin'?" he asks through tears. "Where's Blake goin'?"

"There's somebody else, I think."

"Somebody else . . ." This is her father's moment to come apart, she fears. She had hers earlier, but her father never got the chance. True, he hasn't witnessed half of the nightmares she's been forced to in the past few hours, but he's seen enough. He's heard enough. So she tries to steady her tone, hoping the sound of her voice will be her best tool for securing him to his own bones.

"Somebody else responsible for John's murder. He was alone with one of those ba—" She wants to call them bastards, but that seems profane given their terrible fate. "Those *men* on the roof before the guy got took. And he must have . . . I don't know. He must've said something to him about there being somebody else involved. Why else would Blake take the vines with him?"

"You think he's gonna kill whoever it is?"

"He thinks he doesn't have long to live. So he's gonna do something he wouldn't do otherwise. I don't know . . . I don't know what . . ."

"So which is it gonna be, baby?" Willie finally asks her. "We gonna run or we gonna burn this place?"

"These things don't burn. We start a fire and we might just set 'em all free."

"So we run?"

"I don't know, Daddy."

"Oh, Nova, I know you always hated this place—"

170

"Daddy, don't. You don't have to . . . Not right now. You don't—"

"This is *your* house, Nova."

She's sure it's just a figure of speech, or that some swell of emotion twisted his words at the last moment, so she keeps closing the distance between them. But he holds up both hands to stop her, his palms white as bone in the darkness: "Nova. It's your house."

"What?" she whispers.

He straightens, clears his throat, and appears to test his sure-footed stance, like he fears she'll try to knock him off his feet when he explains further.

"I know I kept you here longer than you ever wanted to be. I know as soon as you started reading those books 'bout slave days that all you saw in this place was the blood of our brothers and sisters everywhere. And I hoped one day you could forgive this house and Miss Caitlin and people who don't know no better 'bout their own history."

"I don't understand, Daddy. Why?"

"Because if Miss Caitlin's really gone . . . then this place . . . it belongs to you . . . 'Cause when I tried to leave last year, when I was gonna start my own bidness wit yer uncle, she told me to name my price. And that was my price. Spring House. For *you*. I never in a million years thought she'd say yes, but she did. And then when I thought about it, it done made some sense 'cause Miss Caitlin, she didn't want this place. Neither did Troy. She's got her money and all kinds of things. This was her daddy's dream. But you . . . I figured the land alone could set you up for life, if she said yes. So I told her she'd have to leave it to you."

"And you never thought she would."

"No. I thought I'd strike out on my own like you always wanted. Maybe finally earn your respect."

"You always had my respect."

"Maybe so, baby girl. Maybe so. But do I have it now?" His voice is quaking, and she can see his jaw quivering in the flashlight's glow. "Do I have it now that you know what I've left you? Land with nothing but evil under it?"

She answers by embracing him, and when she feels his wet sobs against her shoulder, she tightens her hold. *Mine,* she thinks. *This house, this land . . . it's mine.* And this knowledge seems to radiate up her legs from the earth itself, warming her belly and filling her with newfound energy. But that's all. On an ordinary night, Nova would be ecstatic over this news. But tonight these ideas feel like vague abstractions, and what she feels is a sudden, quieting sense of responsibility.

Without meaning to, Nova has angled the Maglite's beam at the ruined gazebo, where a large fresh tendril has emerged from the opening. There are four blossoms lining its thick stalk and they are opening now, the luminescence within intensifying as the white petals spread. Each blossom is about three times the size of the ones inside the house, the swollen mothers of those deceptively beautiful death markers in the front parlor and ruined study.

Nova pulls gently free of her father's grip. When he sees the new growth in the gazebo, Willie grabs her shoulder. But instead of going still, she reaches up and takes his hand so that they can approach the gazebo together. By the time they're standing at the edge of the swollen crater, the radiance from the opening blossoms is enough to see by, and Nova has lowered the Maglite to one side, its beam no longer necessary to guide them.

All sides of the crater are now draped with thick, blossom-lined vines, the petals on each opening with something that looks like leisurely anticipation. But what nails Nova in place is the sight waiting for them at the bottom of the pit, the swelling green protrusion that's pushing its way gradually up from the bottom. A few seconds of staring at it, and Nova realizes it's merely a semitranslucent skin over a dark, shadowy mass within.

"It's a pod, isn't it?" Nova asks.

"Yeah . . ."

Blake is right. It's a process they're paying witness to, and it was set in motion by Caitlin's blood, and then by Blake's blood, and since then its individual components have proven themselves impervious to fire, and possibly a dozen other forms of physical destruction.

"There's something inside that thing," Willie whispers.

"I know."

"And it's growing. Right now. In front of us."

"I know, Daddy."

"We can't let it. Whatever's inside that thing, we can't jes let it—"

"I know. But we can't burn it. Not when it's . . . like this."

"Let's try."

"And burn down the whole damn house?"

"Then, what? We jes run?"

"No."

"I'm not gettin' it, baby. What's the plan here?"

"We wait for it to be born," she answers. "*Then* we burn it."

The gazebo is quiet now, the blossoms open—eighteen in all, Nova's counted—and her father's astonished, frightened glare is raising hairs on the back of her neck.

"You sure?" he asks, when she finally looks him in the eye.

"About which part? The waiting or the burning?"

"Both."

"Yeah, I'm sure."

They hear it at the same time, a sound like flying chain saws, and the expression on Nova's face is enough to make her father grab her by the wrist and take off running. The sound gets louder as they

173

run straight into the empty, unplanted fields, and after a few minutes of not feeling a bug or anything like it on her skin, Nova risks a look over one shoulder.

They aren't being pursued. The cloud of insects sweeping down out of the sky is headed straight for the gazebo, and the shadows they make as they flit through the security light above the kitchen door are the size of sparrows. These aren't the insects that have been gathering inside the house, awaiting the call of whatever strange power pulses inside of the death blossoms. These are the terrible obsidian monsters that left only an hour before. And now they're back.

Nova finally stops running. Her father pulls on her for a few tugs before he gives in and stops running too. Chests heaving, both bent over with hands braced on their knees so they can catch their breath, Nova and Willie watch as the insect cloud descends on the gazebo's wreckage. The collective glow from the blossoms illuminates the great swirling cloud of monstrous bugs. Then the glow itself is extinguished as the bugs pile onto each large flower, coating it with a greater speed and ferocity than exhibited by any of their smaller forebears who have taken up residence inside the main house.

"Mother of God," Willie whispers. "Whatever's in that gazebo, they're *pollinatin'* it."

They're transfixed by the play of shadows around the gazebo's tilting ruins, when suddenly a fierce flicker illuminates the front parlor. To Nova it looks like a small, contained lightning storm. They're too far from the house to see the chandelier in any detail, but she's sure that's the source. She's sure that the bugs gathered around its dangling crystals are on the move, taking the next step of this unholy process that's turned the property before them into a launching pad for winged demons.

The sound of shattering glass from the front parlor is loud enough to mean at least two of the front windows have just been broken through. And when she realizes the violent little electrical storm has ceased, Nova whispers Blake's name and grips her father's right hand.

"Nova—"

"We're stayin'. This is my house now and I'm sick of this shit."

Her father just stares at her, and she can't tell if it's exhaustion or shock that's drained any discernible expression from his face. "Well, all right," he finally says. "Then I'm gonna get us some help."

32

Blake has seen the outside of Vernon Fuller's house before, but he's never had the nerve to cross the entrance to the long driveway. The place was once the family's modest weekend retreat, but ever since Vernon abandoned his wife and his career, it's become his permanent refuge. In other parts of Des Allemands, this one-story L of weathered red brick would be just another unimpressive tract house, but the lot here has frontage on a secluded, tree-lined corner of the bayou, and the boat dock floating in the inky water looks taller than the house itself.

The 1988 Suburban, the same vehicle Blake so often finds waiting for him outside the hospital where he works, is parked at the head of the driveway, its chunky nose kissing the half-open door to a garage that looks like it's been turned into some kind of toolshed or workroom.

By the time he reaches the front door, the tree frogs and crickets are accelerating their frantic song in anticipation of sunrise, and he wonders if their music will mask the approach of his fate.

He knocks and hears voices from a television inside. They make it impossible to hear whether or not someone is approaching the door from the other side, so when it opens suddenly, Blake finds himself standing almost nose to nose with Vernon Fuller. Both men jerk back, but it's too late for Vernon to hide the revolver he's got in his right hand. He's got no choice but to act tough; he tucks it firmly in the waistband of his jeans, at the small of his back.

"Can I come in?" Blake asks.

The man once had an angry, seductive slant to his eyes that used to remind Blake of the handsome Eastern European politicians he sometimes glimpsed on cable news. But like most of his facial features, it has collapsed some with age, giving him a perpetual suspicious squint. He's wearing jeans and work boots and a white tank top that displays the lingering huskiness of a former athlete, and it's clear Blake has disturbed him in the middle of getting dressed.

Blake smells coffee, not the stink of hard alcohol, and the living room behind Vernon is cluttered but not the reality-show ruin Blake had hoped for. The fact that Vernon Fuller isn't living in his own filth as penance for his sins, that he's preparing for his day like some normal commuter, fills Blake with a rage that drives him to cross the threshold without being officially invited.

Beneath his shirt, the vine clutches his chest more tightly, thirsty for the hot pulse of anger in his veins.

A wall of sliding glass doors looks out onto the plain swell of grass that tapers down to the water's edge, and in the corner of the living room the WWL *Eyewitness Morning News* plays on a boxy television piled with unopened bills. Police lights splash a haggard-looking roadside motel, and then the screen fills with the face of some pimply teenager, his jaw tensed as he squints into the harsh glare of a camera light. The reporter just off camera says, "You do realize this story is hard to believe, don't you, sir?"

After the reporter sticks the mic back in his face, the kid answers, "I do. I do realize that and I know what I saw, and what I saw was a lot of bugs killing those people."

"Right. But you're also saying—"

"It was the cheaters," the kid says. Dazed, but slightly perturbed, as if he's being asked to give simple directions once more to an elderly and confused relative. "They killed the cheaters."

There's an empty two-second beat while the reporter gives the kid a chance to recant this insane statement, and the kid does nothing of the kind. Instead he lifts a hand to his forehead to shield his eyes from the camera light but remains rooted in place, ready and willing, it seems, to answer more questions.

Vernon kills the television with the remote, settles into a tattered leather Eames chair, and begins shaking a cigarette out of a rumpled soft pack. On top of a short cabinet just a few inches from his right elbow sits an eight-by-ten photograph of John Fuller, taken only months before he was murdered. Blake knows this because Blake took the photograph, on the levee, not too far from where he was later killed. John is beaming, revealing small, unobtrusive teeth, perfectly aligned by braces he'd shed the year before. It's a smile that crinkles bright eyes with the same beautiful Slavic slant his father lost to old age. His swath of black hair, lightly gelled as it always was, is tossed by the wind off the lake and covers most of his forehead.

"Do you want me to stop?" Vernon asks.

For a second or two, Blake thinks he's referring to the cigarette he's just lit. He exhales smoke through both nostrils like a parody of a dragon, but his glassy-eyed stare searches Blake's face even through the cloud.

"My . . . *visits*, I mean," he continues. "Is that why you're here? You want me to stop?"

Blake had planned to take his time and uncover as many more secrets as he could. But the news report just reminded him he doesn't really know how much time he's got left. An hour? Two or three more? They will come for him out of the sky, and they will take him just like they took Caitlin. And if Vernon Fuller fails the test Blake is about to lay out for him, he will be forced to watch, which isn't exactly what Blake wants, but it will be better than nothing.

With a start, Vernon realizes he's sitting on his own gun—that he failed to remove the revolver from the back of his pants before he sat down. He eases forward slightly, eyes on Blake, and pulls the gun free. Blake expects him to slide it in a drawer, but instead he sets it atop the cabinet nearby, just inches from John's photo. He does, however, take care to turn the barrel so that it isn't pointing directly at Blake.

"I know why you come and see me at work," Blake says.

"Do you?"

"Yes. You killed your son."

Vernon Fuller's eyes water. First his lips purse so tightly it's as if he's pressed one finger to them, and then his jaw tightens so much his chin quivers in response. His hands are resting on his knees, but he's leaning forward as if at any second he might propel himself out of his chair and close his fingers around Blake's throat.

And that will be just fine. Fine, but not perfect. Blake is hoping for a gunshot, because a gunshot will unleash enough blood to feed the vine on his chest. Because that's the deal Blake has made with himself, to confront Vernon with what he knows, and allow Vernon's response to seal his fate. Not Blake. Not the vines. Not Caitlin. And not the furious ghost of Virginie Lacroix. No one but Vernon should decide his fate. It might not be the justice of the earth the slaves at Spring House saw before they escaped its destruction, but it's as close as Blake can get in the final hours before he's ripped from this world.

But Vernon Fuller hasn't reached for the gun, or even moved an inch. Blake takes a step toward him, grateful when the glare from a nearby lamp moves across John's framed and frozen smile.

"Mike Simmons. Kyle Austin. The other one . . ."

"Fauchier," Vernon answers in a whisper. "Scott . . . Scott Fauchier."

"Yes. They're dead. All three of them."

"You? Did . . . you?"

"Yes. I killed them."

Is it a lie? Worse, is it a betrayal of the promise Blake made to himself, not to deceive Vernon into spilling blood? It feels like the truth. It feels as if he murdered those three men. Was there something in Blake's soul that wanted those men torn limb from limb, and did the vines consume it and follow its instructions? Could they have done their terrible work without his rage?

Scott Fauchier, he thinks suddenly. *The vines killed Scott Fauchier and I didn't even know who he was, went most of my life never trusting my instinct that there'd been a third assailant, a third killer, so it wasn't possible for me to hate that man in my heart. Or in my blood. I couldn't even tell you what he looked like. I only knew his name because Kyle Austin said it to me on the roof, before the vines tore him apart. Because the vines knew. The crime was written in my blood somehow. And that's why they killed Scott Fauchier too. But the vines knew what he'd done, because his crime was written in my blood somehow. So they knew and they went for him.*

Vernon is waiting for Blake to strike, and when he doesn't the man reaches for his revolver with a tentative, shaking hand. He doesn't aim the gun at Blake with a killer's confidence. Rather, he draws the handle close to his stomach. The barrel trembles.

"You don't know why I come," Vernon finally says. "You've got no idea why."

"You picked the guys on your team you knew would say yes. Then you told them where John and I were meeting and you told them to—"

"I told them to *scare* you!" Vernon roars. "You two, I thought it was just some kind of game. I thought if you didn't have anywhere to *go* that you'd just . . . you'd just *move on*!"

"John was terrified of you finding out. All you had to do was tell him you knew. He would have freaked and called the whole thing off."

"That's not true. The way he looked at you. I knew—from the way . . . I just . . . I wanted to scare you guys. That's all. I told them just to make you feel *scared* so that you wouldn't feel so . . . *comfortable* meeting there, just a few blocks from—"

"You liar!" Blake roars. "You wanted them to beat it out of us! You wanted them to punish us!"

Thunderstruck, Vernon gazes at Blake as if he's tripled in size. He can't tell if it's his volume or his words that have stunned Vernon. The man's gun hand is shaking, the barrel still held close to his stomach as if he plans to muffle any kickback with his own girth. And Blake's fear that the gun might go off accidentally is just a brief spike that gives way to a kind of drowsy satisfaction. He's beyond such petty concerns now. A marked man has no such fears. A man with only hours to live is free to pursue his own final designs and no one else's. And so he digs deeper, urging Vernon's finger to end this for both of them.

"Did you give them a choice at least? Did you threaten them? Or bribe them?"

Instead of answering, though, Vernon asks, "How did you kill them?"

"Magic."

"Uh-huh. OK then. How did you find out?"

"More magic."

"Is that how you're gonna kill me? *Magic?* 'Cause you sure as hell don't have a gun. Otherwise you would have drawn it by now."

"Did you know they were being blackmailed?"

"Yes."

"But you weren't?"

"No."

"Why not?"

"Because they were idiots."

"What does that mean?"

"It means Simmons called me. He actually *called* me after he murdered my son and the cop put the bite on him. And I recorded every goddamn thing he said. And I told him if he or any of those other boys ever mentioned my name, I'd send the tape to the police. So he could take his pick. Me or the cop. All the cop wanted was a piece of their spending money once a month. That was chump change to those little fucking brats. Me? I would have destroyed their lives with a phone call. They were idiots, is what they were."

"They were teenagers."

"They were murderers! You were *there*. You saw."

"Because *you* put them up to it!"

"I put them up to being bullies because that's what they were. That's what I saw in them every day on the field. I didn't know Simmons's dad had messed with him when he was a kid. I didn't know he was going to lose it when he saw you kissing my son."

"Of course you knew. That's why you picked him. You just thought he'd be smart enough to lose it with *me*."

Vernon slumps back into his leather chair, resting the gun on his right thigh, his grip on the handle weak, the barrel pointed in Blake's general direction but aimed at nothing in particular. Suddenly he has the vacant look of a nursing-home patient hollowed out by old age and isolation. Blake can't tell if this is an admission, or the man's just given up fighting with him. But now he needs it—he needs Vernon to shoot him. Needs his revenge. And so he keeps pushing.

"Why do you come visit me once a month then?"

182

"Because seeing you makes me want to die," he answers quietly. "So I wait for you to come out those doors, and if the sight of you still hurts as bad as it did the last time, I come back here." He raises the gun and pops the cylinder out. "I load one bullet." He pops the cylinder back in and presses the revolver's barrel to his right temple. "And I let God decide if I should live."

Vernon keeps the gun pressed to his temple, and for a while the two men just stare at each other as dawn's first light slides across the floorboards between them.

Finally, Vernon says, "Is that good enough for you, Blake Henderson?"

"No."

"Maybe it's time for your *magic* then."

When Blake lifts up the front of his shirt, Vernon's snarl collapses into a vacant, slack-jawed stare. In one hand Blake peels the snake of vine from his chest. It clings to him for a few seconds, but without so much resistance, and in another second or two, he's holding it out for Vernon to see. When it starts to wrap around his wrist, Blake hurls it to the floor. Both ends curl and it starts inchworming toward Blake's feet. He takes a few steps back to lengthen its journey so Vernon can see it in action. The man has lifted his legs up onto his chair, like a parody of a housewife freaking out over a mouse in her kitchen.

"Shoot it," Blake says.

Vernon's lips are trembling; the sight of this otherworldly organism moving across the floor of his home has rattled him out of his guilt, self-loathing, and suicidal fantasizing. And Blake enjoys the sight of this, knowing that he doesn't need to necessarily kill him to get retribution. *If it's all I can do to him, then let me. In the time I have I'll destroy what's left of his sanity by forcing him to bear witness to the horrors I've seen during the long and terrible night.*

"Shoot it, Vernon."

Vernon fires. His aim is good. But it's as if the bullet has been captured by a pocket of electrical energy just a few inches above the vine. There's a spitting arc of flame where the bullet seems absorbed by the vine itself. The vine goes suddenly still, but it's undamaged.

When Blake realizes his ears are ringing so loudly he won't be able to hear the insects coming for him, he feels a swell of genuine panic he can't ignore. He waits another few seconds for the ringing to lessen some; then he starts talking loud enough to hear himself over the din.

"You feed them your blood, you see. They drink from you, and then they devour the people who've hurt you the worst. My friend discovered them. And then she gave them my blood too, and they killed Mike Simmons and Kyle Austin and Scott Fauchier."

"Why didn't they kill me then?"

"I'd have to feed them again. It's a cycle, you see. Which makes sense, after all. It's a plant."

"*That* is *not* a fucking *plant*."

"I know."

"Well . . . are you going to feed it?"

"No."

Vernon takes his eyes off the slack vine for the first time since Blake pulled it from his chest. "Why not?"

"Because I'm not a murderer, Vernon."

Vernon stands and walks to the spot where the vine has gone still.

"If it's a cycle, how does it end?" he asks.

"There's a price . . ."

"What kind of price?"

"Bugs."

"Bugs?" Despite what he's seen with the vine, Vernon can't keep the skepticism out of his voice.

"After they kill, they leave a flower in place of the person's body, and then the bugs come and they feed off it and it changes them. And then they come for the person who gave their blood."

"And then what?"

"They tear them apart."

"You're out of your fucking mind, kid."

"Shoot it again and then tell me I'm crazy. But look me in the eye when you say it."

"So they're coming for you? The *bugs*? They're going to come *here* for *you*?"

"Something like that. Yeah."

"You've seen this? You've *seen* this happen?"

"I've seen all of it."

"And they'll hurt me too?"

"No. It doesn't work like that."

Vernon is distracted by something at Blake's feet, and Blake looks down and sees the vine has wrapped itself around his right ankle.

"Then what the fuck are you doing here?" Vernon asks.

"I wanted to give you a choice."

"'Cause if I'd hurt you, then that thing—that thing will drink your blood and come after me . . ."

"Yes."

When Blake looks up again, Vernon is holding the revolver's handle out to him, and it takes a few seconds of stunned silence for him to realize the man is actually offering him his weapon.

Is he offering Blake the opportunity to kill him? Or is he trying to give him a chance to end his own life before a million winged terrors come for him?

Maybe both. But these questions lodge in his throat when he hears the sound he's been dreading for over an hour now. Here on the bayou, dappled now with the gray light of early dawn, it would be far too easy to pretend it was just the whine of an approaching outboard motor, but Blake knows that isn't true.

He turns to the walls of glass in time to see the great clouds swooping low over the tree line across the bayou. Two matching columns of dark, tumbling flecks barreling straight for the house. One instant they're vivid against the gray sky; then they're camouflaged by the backdrop of the surrounding foliage, even as their whine gets louder.

He can hear Vernon backing away, can hear the man's shuffling, panicked footsteps squeaking against the floorboards.

"I said no," Blake whispers.

He presses his hands to the glass. The clouds cross the water's edge yards away, filling the gaps in between his fingers.

"I said no and you took my blood anyway!" he growls. Who is he praying to? He's not sure. God? Virginie Lacroix? Vernon Fuller?

The whine is deafening now, as loud as it was in the moments before Caitlin was rocketed across the second-floor hallway of Spring House.

"I said no!" Blake screams.

A tremendous force slams into the wall of sliding doors, shattering them in a single eruption powerful enough to send Blake skittering backward. But the hand he held against the glass when it was still intact is still out before him, bloodied, but still rigid and defiant, like a child's attempt to stop an ocean wave. Blake forces his eyes open against the onslaught and sees the clouds have stopped their relentless assault. A thin finger of them reaches almost to the center of his palm, but nothing pricks the skin there, nothing touches his skin at all, and behind this buzzing tendril the clouds are branching off in different directions, a great swirl that extends from the lawn outside through the wall of shattered glass and into the living room.

Is it possible? Has he really staved them off with a single cry and an outstretched palm? Could Caitlin have done the same?

The cloud before him assumes a fibrous shape that is gaining human proportions. The noise they make is steadier and even-toned. Behind him, Vernon Fuller emits desperate panting that sounds almost sexual, if not for the terror pulsing through each one. And a few feet in front of Blake, a face appears out of the insect swarm in impressionistic brushstrokes.

Does the spirit driving these tiny creatures feel compelled to present some random face Blake will find knowable? Or is this monster about to reveal its true identity?

He has never seen a painting or a photograph of Virginie Lacroix. But it doesn't matter, because the face swirling before him now is not hers. The high-domed forehead, the deeply recessed brow, the lips so fat they appear to be peeling free of his face—they are familiar features he's stared up at in the foyer of Spring House since he was a small boy. Blake finds himself staring not at the visage of a murdered slave, but at the face of Spring House's owner.

"Felix . . . ," Blake whispers.

"Blake Henderson."

33

The spirit's voice is so loud it rattles Blake's teeth and every other hard surface in the wrecked living room.

"Who are you?" Blake cries.

"My visage is not intended to deceive."

"You're really Felix Delachaise. You're his—you're his *ghost*?"

"I am what remains of him when he is called back to this plane again and again by the will of another."

The whine of each insect forms a lone note in a monstrous symphony that rattles Blake's bones. It feels as if he and Vernon are literally swimming in the spirit's every word.

"Who brought you back? Caitlin?"

"You and Caitlin Chaisson are the tools, nothing more."

"The tools for what?"

"My freedom. My existence consists of teasing glimpses of a realm of limitless possibility before I am returned again and again to the soil of this earthly plane, the soil beneath Spring House. There I am forced to endure the racket of human passion and rage. Ever since the death of my body, I have poked and prodded at your meager existences from my prison of spirit and blossoms, desperate for a way to unburden myself of

my sins, so that I may move on. Know this. It is not the living who are haunted by the dead—it is the dead who are haunted by the living."

"I don't understand. The will of another . . . whose will? Who keeps bringing you back?"

"Life, human life, is nothing but resistance to the infinite. All cells, all spirits, are without shelter, are without home, until they find a single will around which they may gather and take form. And as long as that will endures, there is life, even if it doesn't wear a costume of flesh and bone. And so, as long as Virginie Lacroix's will to walk this earth as a free woman endures, I am tasked with her resurrection. I am doomed to live as the slave to my slave."

"All life?" Blake cries. "You're saying anyone can be brought back if they didn't want to die?"

"Those with magic in their hands do not die as easily as others might."

Blake feels again the soft bed that was waiting for him at the bottom of the pit when he jumped into it to cut a segment of the vines free. A new growth, a new life, swelling up from the earth itself in response to the terrible events all around Spring House.

"We're the tools you're using to bring her back?"

"Yes."

"How?"

"Betrayal is my sin. I used Virginie Lacroix's powers for gain and refused to keep my promises to her in exchange. Her revenge caused my death and took prisoner of my spirit. But I was given new direction and new power by the blood of Caitlin Chaisson and the betrayal that ran through it. Her rage. This is the justice of the earth."

"Rage? That's the *essence* of life itself? Only rage?"

"All life? Perhaps not. Perhaps only the life I am able to create while trapped in this prison. The life I am able to create for Virginie."

"But you stopped," Blake says. "You just stopped. Why haven't you taken me?"

The spirit doesn't answer. The low whine from the surrounding insects could be their usual song or Felix's frustrated growl; there's no telling which.

"Where's Caitlin?"

"What remains of Caitlin has gathered up the lives she needs to aid me in the resurrection. She has returned to Spring House to play her role."

"And now it's my turn to play mine? Is that it? You've come for me and then I'll . . . what?"

"You will devour more of the sin that fed your rage, the same rage with which you fed the vines. And then you too will play your role in Virginie's resurrection . . ."

"And your freedom, right? Because when you bring Virginie back to life, you'll be free? Is that how this all works?"

There is no response from the clicking, shifting apparition, but there is no clearly etched facial expression to interpret either, so Blake takes the silence of this ghost as hesitation, a gap in the all-seeing divine knowledge it touted only seconds before.

"Fine!" Blake shouts. "Then do it! Do it now!"

And yet, the spirit is silent. The swirl of insects, not a single one of which touches his skin, now seems stuck in a kind of repetitive paralysis.

"You can't. Why not? Why can't you take me the way you took Caitlin?"

The spirit's form is too impressionistic for Blake to read any emotion or nuance from its vague expression.

Vernon has collapsed in the far corner, a few feet from the Eames chair he knocked over as he stumbled backward. Squinting, his chest heaving, he sweeps the curtains of winged, otherworldly creatures with a swaying, indecisive aim.

"It matters," Blake whispers. "The choice I made. That I said *no.* It matters, doesn't it? It's stopped you."

"It has done more than that, I'm afraid."

"What? What . . . *more* has it done?" Blake is answered by the grinding buzz, but not words. "Caitlin screamed bloody murder, but *she* couldn't stop you. How come I can? What happened when you took my blood, my *rage*, without my consent?"

"It placed me under your command."

Vernon aims the gun at Blake. A piss stain crawls down the right leg of his jeans.

"I want you to stop," Blake says. "If you're under my *command* now, then *stop!*"

"There is no stopping Virginie's desire for freedom, and there is no freeing me from it until she is made flesh again. No matter what you choose, I will be returned to the soil, forced to await another opportunity to gain her freedom and mine, but with the knowledge I have acquired during this long night of consumption and enlightenment."

"Why don't you have enough? Why haven't you . . . *enough* to bring her back? You killed all those people at the motel, didn't you? That was part of this."

"Caitlin's rage killed those people."

"They were cheaters, like Troy. Is that it?"

"She consumed the sin she sought to avenge. She is but one of my arms. She fed but one of my vines. You fed the other."

"No. You did. You *stole* my blood, and now you're being punished for it!"

"I am the prisoner of the vines, not their architect."

For the first time since this sickening dialogue has begun, Blake lowers his outstretched hand and decides to put his alleged power to the test a second time. Under his command, the countenance of Felix Delachaise collapses, and within seconds the mass of insects has formed a smooth, undulating blanket covering the living room ceiling. It looks like smoke from a well-fed fire, but the constant grinding song of its indistinguishable components belies the soft texture of the swarm's new configuration. A configuration that resembles exactly what Blake envisioned for it only seconds before.

Staring up at the blanket of insects overhead, Vernon seems to realize his gun will be useless against Blake's newfound power, and when he lowers it to one side, the placid expression on his face reminds Blake of a patient who realizes she is close enough to death to abandon all fight.

"Do it, Blake."

"No . . . ," Blake says.

"Come on, kid," Vernon answers. His smile makes him look delirious, and Blake wonders if this is the way Vernon used to talk to his son. He wonders if, in a part of his mind that's already separated from the body he's offering up now as sacrifice, Vernon really is talking to John. If that's who he sees standing across the wrecked room from him now. "No need to pretend for my sake. I know you want to. And it makes sense, doesn't it? It makes perfect sense to give me to the—"

"Shut up!"

"You were a hero once, Blake," he says, shattering Blake's cozy notion that Vernon no longer knows who he is. "You could have left him. You could have just started swimming, but you tried—you tried to get my son free before he drowned. You really loved him, didn't you?"

"Stop . . . Please, just st—"

"Did you love him?"

"*Yes!*"

"I see . . . Well, I *didn't*," he growls, but there are tears sprouting from his eyes and a childlike quiver to his lower jaw, and Blake can see it's just a performance. "I wanted him to die. I wanted you both to die."

"That's not true. You're just saying that to make me—"

"It *is* true. I thought you were sick, both of you. I thought you were both diseased." But there is no rage behind these words, just tearful despair. *"I wanted you both to die!"*

Blake realizes he's shaking his head madly only when his neck starts to burn from the effort. Vernon is simply parroting the script Blake just gave him, that's all—making himself out to be the monster Blake wanted him to be when he knocked on the front door.

"You're just saying that to make me—"

Vernon hits one knee and grabs his gun before Blake can finish the sentence. There is madness in Vernon's eyes beyond calculation or reason.

Vernon fires.

Blake hits his knees, feels the bullet whiz past his shoulder. The insects overhead don't react to the gunshot itself; they are attuned only to the gunfire within Blake's soul, and Blake is trying with all his might not to will Vernon's death, not to end things in this way, no matter how tempting, no matter how easy it seems.

Deafened by the gunshot, Blake doesn't hear the gun hit the wood next to him, just sees it spinning away across the floor, and he doesn't realize Vernon has lunged until the man's weight comes crashing down on him.

They hit the floor together in a tangle of limbs, catching one side of the glass coffee table on their way down. Ashtrays and magazines tumble across Vernon's back, and the next thing Blake knows, Vernon Fuller's got him by both shoulders and is slamming the back of his head against the floor. The words rip from him in a torrent of furious growls. In the air behind Vernon's head, the insects fly in mad circles like shocked witnesses, powerless to intervene without Blake's command.

"Die, you faggot! *Die!*" Vernon roars. "It should have been you! It should have been you. *I wanted you to die!*"

It's not true. None of it's true and Blake knows it. But the gunshot hasn't worked, and so now Vernon has to make Blake believe he's willing to kill him. Now Vernon must convince Blake there's no choice but to sacrifice him to Felix Delachaise's hungry, winged minions. And then, even as it feels like he's still debating this terrible question, something inside of Blake gives way. Amid the racket all around them—Vernon's growls, curses, and slurs mingling with the steady whine of the bugs covering the ceiling—Blake can't know if he's whispered the words aloud, but he certainly thinks them.

Take him . . .

The insistent buzz throttles down into a deeper, throatysounding whine, and a column of insects flies into Vernon's open mouth, lifting him several feet into the air, where the remainder of the cloud closes in around him and the raw material of his human form is peeled away from him quickly and bloodlessly.

Blake hits the floor knees-first, then goes over, the sobs ripping from him but impossible to hear over the angry roar above. The sound changes again, from a riot of motorboats to a flock of chain saws, and a few of the little monsters clatter off the floor on all sides of him before rejoining their brothers and sisters overhead. But when Blake looks up, a blinding light seems to spread across the entire house, reflected equally off the shattered glass doors and the mirrors above the television, and suddenly he is raising both arms, as the buzz-saw sound of the insects is replaced by something that sounds more like a man's rageful scream.

34

When he sees Blake approaching down the front walk, the black man standing guard on the front porch of Spring House takes a few steps forward, his hand drifting to the gun at his hip. But his expression remains fixed and stern. The sight of Blake, scratched and bleeding, his shirt torn in a dozen different places from Vernon Fuller's last, desperate attempt to make Blake believe he was trying to kill him, can't hold a candle to whatever this man has just witnessed.

"Willie? Nova?" They are the first words Blake has uttered since his conversation with a ghost, and before the man can answer, there's a scream from somewhere behind the house that causes him to flinch, but just slightly. This isn't the first time the man before him has been subjected to the strange intermingling of voices joined together in a high, sharp cry, almost like train wheels coming to a sudden, grinding halt.

"You Blake?" the man asks. His voice trembles, and so, Blake sees, does the hand resting tentatively atop his gun. Now Blake recognizes him as one of Willie's good friends, part of the usual crew Willie conscripted to work Caitlin's parties over the years. His fear is palpable, and the closer Blake gets to him, the more he can see the man's injuries are much like his own: claw marks that look like they were left by a human across his right forearm, bruises on his face and neck.

The early morning light splashes the tops of the oak trees overhead, and soon the extent of Spring House's injuries will be revealed to the day. One section of banister and railing on the widow's walk has completely collapsed, right at the spot where Kyle Austin was pulled straight through the roof by the vines.

Not the vines, he corrects himself. *Felix. Felix Delachaise. Felix, who is now . . . what, exactly?*

The soaring front windows are shattered, as are all the slender ones framing the front door. The columns nearest the door are flecked with the impacts of the swarm that carried away Caitlin Chaisson's very essence, her very soul. And in the middle of it all stands a proud, terrified black man whose last visit to the place was to serve rich white people, and who is now trying not to betray that he has just borne witness to things that have perverted his view of reality.

"Willie says if you came, I was to bring you inside," the man says.

Blake nods, and follows him from a polite distance, hoping that allowing him to take the lead will settle the man more firmly in his skin, and settle his mind once again.

The foyer is still a ruin, only now that portrait of Felix has finally tumbled from its perch, the canvas speared on one corner of a chest of drawers.

And then the screams come again. Not as piercing or devastating as the final wail he heard inside Vernon's house as creatures under Blake's command consumed the man. This sound has a more frustrated, aspirational quality. More like an engine trying to start up, an engine composed of several different high-pitched and desperate voices. And this time, it's followed by a great crash.

All evidence of the devouring of Mike Simmons has been scrubbed from the giant front parlor, and through the open back door Blake sees Willie's back. He is seated on the top step, rocking gently back and forth with his hands crossed over his stomach. Flanking him are two other men, also friends of Willie's he recognizes from having worked various parties over the years, both armed, both gazing out at the ruined gardens before them with vacant, thousand-yard stares and small blood-dappled injuries on their arms and faces.

The spot where the gazebo once stood is now a yawning crater lined with great withered leaves. The crater is twice as deep as it was when Blake jumped down into it to cut free a section of vine just hours before. It appears as if a single event drained the life from all the impossible plant structures that had been pushing their way through it for a day, and now they're strewn about the crater, fossilized remnants of a recent event. Much of the garden has been destroyed by what look like the claw marks of a great winged beast struggling to take flight. It makes Blake long in an almost nostalgic way for the small upsets and upended fountain Nova pointed out to him the day before.

The screams rend the air again.

They've come from the shed, where a cloud of black insects puffs through fresh cracks in the roof and walls. Something slams into the shed's front wall from inside, and that's when Blake sees Nova. His first thought is that she's dead and for some reason they have chained her by both wrists to the door of the shed. The exhalation that comes from him turns into a defeated-sounding moan, which causes Willie to glance in his direction and then shoot to his feet when he sees it's Blake. And by the time Willie has grabbed him by his shoulders, Blake sees Nova is very much alive, gritting her teeth. When the door behind her bucks from the impact of some powerful force within, Nova rears up, feet planted on the soil, upper back sealed to the door, turning herself into a human doorstop.

"Second swarm never came back," Willie's whispering, with the speed and breathlessness of someone nearly mad. "First one, one that took Caitlin, came back right after you left. Bet it killed all those people at that motel first. Then it came back here, went straight for the gazebo. But the second one. The second one . . ."

Blake knows what Willie is asking. Did Blake manage to outrun them, or have the bugs yet to catch up to him?

"It's over," Blake whispers.

There's another series of screams from the shed, another impact against the walls that causes Nova to let out a startled bark and lift her butt up off the ground to straighten her bound arms.

"It ain't over," says one of the men next to him.

Blake is having trouble finding his words. "Why did you—"

"We didn't do that," Willie says, gesturing toward his daughter. "We had a deal. We had a plan. We was gonna kill whatever was born out of that damn thing, whatever came out of the gazebo we was going to blow it to hell, set it on fire, anything we could do. We wasn't gonna let it loose on the world, that's for sure." The smell of kerosene hits Blake, and that's when he sees the small trenches they dug around the gazebo, trenches they never managed to light, otherwise Blake's eyes wouldn't be watering from the fumes. "But it looked like some slave woman, and that's when Nova . . . that's when Nova took the chain we was gonna use if we had to tie whatever it was down, and she chased it into the shed, and she did that to her wrists and swallowed the key." Tears sprout from Willie's bloodshot eyes, and the arm with which he's been gesturing wildly to his daughter flies to his mouth.

"I'll talk to her," Blake says quietly.

The absence of fear in his voice startles him as much as it does the other men. When he steps down off the porch, he hears one of them following and figures it's Willie.

Nova is staring down at her lap as he approaches, her chest rising and falling with deep breaths, her narrowed eyes and tense jaw a study in strained concentration amid terror. When she sees Blake standing a few feet away, what appears to be a drunken smile passes over her face.

"Hot damn," she says, her voice hoarse from a night of screams. "Hot damn, look who made it."

"What are you doing, Nova?" he asks as gently as he can.

"Just giving it some time, that's all. Because that's all she needs. *Time.*"

"It ain't a she!" Willie barks. "It's all sorts of people in one. It don't *know* what it is."

Nova ignores her father's cry, blinks madly, and tries to study Blake closely.

"So what'd you do, Blake? You outrun them?"

"No."

"Burn them?"

Blake shakes his head. "Where's the key, Nova?"

"She swallowed it," Willie wails. "I tol' you. I'll cut you free, girl. I'm gonna get an axe and cut you free if you don't stop this—"

"I don't have to stop nothing!" Nova's rage is pushing her voice past its limits. She is oblivious to the sliver of drool dripping from one corner of her mouth. "You just have to *wait*. You just have to put your guns down and *wait*, Daddy!"

Her outburst silences them but not the tumult inside the shed. Now that he's close enough, Blake can hear what sounds like the persistent flight of some trapped winged creature. The roof jumps, and then a sidewall, and then the door.

"Seriously," Nova says. "Seriously . . . how are you . . . *alive?*"

"You were right."

"About what?"

"It made a difference. That I said no. You were right, Nova. It made a big difference."

"Well, good." The smile that breaks across Nova's face brings tears to her eyes; his words were a ray of sunshine in a long nightmare of seemingly impenetrable darkness. And he feels himself smiling as well, and then he's blinking back tears too. "Well, that's real good, Blake."

"Yeah. It is . . . I hope."

"It's her, Blake," Nova whispers, jaw quivering. "It's Virginie."

"It's not her!" Willie roars.

"It's her," Blake says quietly.

They both stare at him as if they're sure that whatever he's just experienced outside of Spring House has endowed him with this knowledge and the confidence with which he has expressed it. But for Willie it's still not enough. "Then she's *evil*. Then she's the one who killed those boys! She's the one who took Miss Caitlin and went to that motel and killed all those poor people. They in her now, those people. *They in her now!*"

"Blood gets spilled every time a baby's born," Blake says. "It doesn't make the baby evil."

"Does that thing sound like a baby to you?" Willie asks.

What happens next comes so quickly neither Nova nor Willie has time to process it. There's a brief flash of light that moves so fast Blake is confident he's the only one who saw the trail it made as it swept from behind him and across Nova's wrists. And he was able to see it only because he was expecting it. Then Nova's wrists slip free of the chain that's been cut in half. Its heavy links fall to the mud on either side of her with wet thuds; the broken padlock tumbles free, and suddenly she is lowering her arms in front of her in disbelief.

When Blake extends his hand, she takes it in a daze. He lifts her to her feet, and the door to the shed swings open behind her. Once he's tucked Nova behind him, Blake steps forward into the darkness.

35

Willie and his men must have emptied the shed of most of its supplies before the creature inside emerged from the ground. Whatever the thing is, it's down on all fours like a dog, its bent, misshapen limbs shuddering. The pale morning light falls in thin slats across its back, which appears to be changing color with liquid speed. He can make out two contrasting skin tones, one after the other. First he sees the same rich brown of Nova's and Willie's flesh, then, a few quivering seconds later, the pale and red-blotched skin tone of some white person. They pulse across the thing's outer shell in alternating waves, each with the same brilliance as the luminescence Blake saw in the death-marker blossoms Nova could not burn.

The creature rockets toward the ceiling. For a second, it looks as if the thing has propelled itself skyward on its hind legs. But they are long and tendril-like, incapable of supporting the creature's full weight. The head, which Blake sees for the first time, is vaguely human in shape, but the features are a riot of indecisive transformations, undulations involving musculature and bone. And now the head is thrown back on its long neck, gazing upside down at Blake from the ceiling with wide, expectant eyes and a yawning mouth. The face of a man is there for an instant, a man Blake doesn't recognize—someone from the motel, he figures. But then it leaves like a reflection on water that's been sliced by a skipping stone; the eyes ripple and are gone, leaving socketless caverns of molten bone.

When the creature screams, the sound is so deafening Blake's hands fly to his ears. He hits the dirt floor knees-first. In time with the terrible intermingling cries, two tendrils of insects fly from the creature's half-formed nostrils, tumbling across the empty interior of the shed, bouncing over bare shelves before flying through the cracks in the ceiling and walls.

Shedding. It's the only word Blake can think of to describe what he's witnessing—the lavalike transformations of skin and bone, the entangled screams, the sudden rocketing skyward followed by the eruption of insects from the creature's nose. It's just as Willie said: all the spirits within this creature are fighting for control. All traces of the man he glimpsed seconds before are gone now, and when the creature flips and lands on all fours on the floor a few feet away, Blake finds himself staring into Caitlin's eyes. The rest of her body is a spindly, shuddering mess of naked pale flesh, and her great yawning mouth has no lips, just ragged borders of skin that flap like rubber casing around an air duct.

"Caitlin!" Blake screams.

The eyes meet his, the same eyes that greeted him when he came to in the hospital room after being beaten by John's killers, the same eyes that turned to him in agony and despair when the bugs came for her. Even as the rest of the body shudders and molts and transforms, the vestiges of Caitlin's spirit stare out at him from this impossible war between flesh and dueling spirits.

The sound of her name, and the familiar voice that just screamed it, intensifies Caitlin's hold on the hovering riot of flesh and bone. Blake has the sense that he has just called Caitlin further into being, and he doesn't know if that's what he wants.

The creature rises, but without the same mad propulsion with which it rocketed to the ceiling only moments before. Caitlin's long nose begins to take shape on the creature's face, her eyes—too large to be human but still distinctly hers—widen and grow even larger, and the vague outlines of human lips resolve around the edges of her yawning mouth. Birdlike breasts swell on her chest. He sees her legs for the first time, which dangle behind her like broken tree limbs.

"Caitlin?" Blake asks.

"AmIprettyamIprettyamIprettyamIprettyamIprettyamIpretty amIpretty?"

The words sound like whale song filtered through the same grinding buzz of insects that has terrorized them for most of this long, awful cycle of slaughter and rebirth.

"Let her go!" Nova screams.

When Blake looks over his shoulder, he sees Willie and the other men holding Nova back. Their combined effort has dragged her several feet away from the door to the shed.

Blake looks back to the spirit. More of Caitlin's features now dominate the otherwise misshapen face. Her eyes burn with a familiar rage.

"Caitlin . . . please . . ."

The spirit's eyes meet his.

And Blake is speechless. *Please* . . . What could he say to her? What could she reveal to him that would help him to make the choice he knows comes next?

Show me. Show me you have learned something in death. Show me you have become something better than the self-loathing and the rage that have delivered you to this state and set this nightmare free upon the soil. Show me, Caitlin. Show me you are worth saving. Show me why I shouldn't destroy you with the new power that has been placed in my hands.

Her answer is the same mad, rhythmic plea: *"Ammmmmmmmm IIIIIIIIIIIII prrrrrrreeeeeeettttttttyyyyyyyyyyyy?"*

And he cannot answer. *Is this death?* he thinks. *Is this what we become at the moment of our death, not our purest form, but our basest self?*

From outside the shed, Nova Thomas screams, "Let her go, you bitch!"

The lips vanish from Caitlin's mouth. Once again it's a yawning dark hole, and from it pour two heavy flows of insects, blacker and thicker than any of the earlier eruptions—their constituent parts too tiny to make out, their sound a smooth buzz compared to the night's previous swarms. And as they evacuate the body, Blake watches in astonishment as her skin darkens until it's a light shade of mocha. The limbs become slender and proportional, delicate even. For a few seconds, it appears the great tide of black spirit matter leaving her has also caused the dirt floor to swallow her. But she is simply shrinking down to human size. Her black skin glistens; her delicate facial features are defined enough to give her an expression of astonished surrender as the bugs leave her.

Virginie . . .

Blake is so astonished by the slave woman taking proper form before him, he has paid no attention to the gathering cloud above. Within its dark swirl, a towering and ghostly impression of Caitlin Chaisson has taken shape. Her mad, pupil-less eyes are focused on the astonished gathering just beyond the shed's open door.

Did Virginie Lacroix summon some great reserve of strength and wrest control of her resurrected body from Caitlin's spirit? Or did Caitlin leave her in a divine rage over Nova's last slur? Has Caitlin chosen this form because it will better allow her to tear Nova apart?

There is no mistaking the hatred in the spirit's—*Caitlin's*—eyes. The wall around the shed door shatters. A tide of wet, cold air blasts across Blake's neck. He glimpses Willie hoisting Nova off her feet, one of his arms around her waist, the other holding his shotgun, and the terrified assemblage scrambles desperately up onto the back porch. Then Blake gives Felix Delachaise his first command since ordering him to consume Vernon Fuller.

"Take her!" he cries. "Take her now!"

❧

At the last second, when it's clear they won't be able to outrun the mad ghost made of insects, Willie drops Nova and spins on the advancing spirit, raising his shotgun. Nova's ass slams to the floor of the porch so hard her teeth knock together. But the pain is a dull, distant thing as she stares death in the face.

Nova is ready to die. The rage has left her, and she is filled with a sudden and total comfort over the fact that she will die in defiance of the spirit's rage—of Caitlin's rage. She only wishes the men would leave her to her fate. Not her father. But Sam and Allen. Because this is not something they invited on themselves.

These thoughts are halted by the sight of Blake standing just inside the shed's ruined front wall, a silhouette through the dark gauze of the furious approaching insects. But his hands are at his sides, his fingers splayed, animated, it seems, by an intense power.

The first column of them comes zipping over the roof of the house, glowing so brightly their violent interior light isn't dimmed in the slightest by the rising sun. They are like fireflies that appear out of thin air itself, and they tear through Caitlin's raging, advancing spirit in a fierce bright line, like shrapnel shredding a plane's fuselage. The first column is dotted by white flapping wings, as is the second, which flares across the cracked, shifting roof of the shed before blasting into Caitlin's remnants from behind. It looks as if

206

they are cleaving and incinerating the tiny monsters in the same instant. Compared to what they are attacking, these new luminescent winged saviors move with determination and grace, making a sound like a saw cutting cleanly through wood.

And there's no mistaking Blake's pose, his posture. If he isn't driving these things, he has summoned them somehow. How else to explain his confidence, his stillness, and the steadiness of his outstretched hands?

It made a difference, that I said no. You were right, Nova. It made a difference.

But the battle isn't done. The remaining floating tendrils of Caitlin's mutilated spirit rise, struggling to reassemble. But the fierce blue invaders—they are either dragonflies or the spirit world's imitation of them—are penetrating these columns, matching their every duck and weave until the last dark remnants of Caitlin Chaisson's spirit are being chased skyward, toward the lightening sky and its tufts of clouds.

Only when a silence falls does Nova realize how high the last evidence of this battle has ascended.

She rises to her feet, stumbles down the back steps, eyes skyward, searching for any last remainder of the spirit that almost devoured her. But they are gone, and as the last few sparkling flecks of power Blake called forth wink out in the sky overhead, she sees he has gently closed the fingers on each hand.

And then the watery silence is pierced by a new sound, a sound that in any other circumstance would be alarming enough to elicit at least a grimace from one of the stunned people staring skyward. But in this garden of ruin, it is a comfort. It is full of promise. It is the sound of a woman crying with the confusion and pain of one newly born.

AFTER

The letter finds him in a small town in Arizona called Superior. A few months after he left New Orleans, a stray rock shattered the windshield of his motorcycle, and when he pushed it by both handlebars into the nearest auto body shop, he found himself surrounded by a ghost town cradled in a vast, dry valley, with a boarded-up main street he recognized from various films about the sad and lonely Southwest.

The bike is a Honda ST1300, new and easy to fix, and the Navajo who runs the auto body shop on the edge of town had no trouble getting the replacement parts right away. But within hours of arriving in Superior by accident, Blake was seduced by the stark solemnity of the place. After a few nights at the nearest motel, he looked into renting a trailer on the edge of Queen Creek. He believed, perhaps foolishly, Superior's vast emptiness would give his nightmares enough space in which to roam so they wouldn't crowd him come sunrise.

So far, he's been right.

The website for the local chamber of commerce tries to make a big deal out of the town's geographical location. Superior sits on a dividing line between Arizona's three predominant landscapes:

Sonoran Desert to the west, mineral-rich valleys and plateaus to the south, mountain ranges to the east. On the map he's managed to draw in his mind after half a year of exploring the region on his bike, the eastern half of the state is covered in a giant Do Not Enter sign, its letters dripping red ink. Because with mountains comes denser foliage, even in Arizona. Just the thought of a branch dangling in the air behind his neck causes him to shudder and ball his hands into fists.

He spends most evenings sipping Coronas on the back steps of his trailer and watching the sunset paint the jagged rock faces at the edge of town with deep shades of blood orange and merlot. These rocks and the surrounding arid landscape give him strength, he is sure of it. Enough strength to keep from being frightened of the rattlesnakes that often gather atop the rocks beside the creek. They are fellow confused travelers, that's all, barraged with stimuli that must—to their limited senses, at least—seem supernatural in origin. And besides, the earth under Spring House confronted him with far more determined and calculating sources of fear than some sluggish reptile living out a monotonous ritual of feeding and slumber.

When the letter reaches his doorstep, Blake is not surprised; he uses fake IDs in most circumstances to avoid leaving a trace that could connect him to any of the rare but extraordinary events throughout the Southwest for which he and his shadow, his guardian angel—his *ghost*—are responsible. But the bike is still in his name. He's left this one connection to his previous life in place so that his father's sister might be able to track him down should her health fail as quickly as that of her siblings.

And then there's Nova.

He isn't familiar enough with her handwriting to know if she's the one who wrote his name and address on the envelope. There is, however, a slight hint of her perfume, just strong enough to make him wonder if she scented the letter on purpose. A warning, perhaps. Or proof that she was truly responsible for whatever it contains.

Even though he has no presence online himself, Blake has used library computer labs to check in every now and then on the legal status of the Chaisson estate. Alexander Chaisson installed a combined clause in the trust allowing for transfer of ownership to a board made up of Caitlin's cousins in the event of her disappearance or severe mental incapacitation. And the trust's definition of a disappearance—four months without any verifiable communication between Caitlin and the trust—could be established in considerably less time than the seven years required for a declaration of death in the state of Louisiana.

If Caitlin's cousins have balked at the idea of Spring House passing out of the trust and into the hands of the gardener's only daughter, there was no mention of it in the press. Perhaps, like Willie, Caitlin's relatives had always sensed menace lurking there. *Sideways, all through everything and waiting to be fed,* as Willie had put it.

Or perhaps they had no interest in inheriting the last place Caitlin's husband was seen alive. One thing was for sure: Caitlin's disappearance had enriched her family to a significant degree. In fact, while most other families would have spent their time at the police station demanding that their loved one be found, Caitlin's family had spent that time at their lawyers' offices arranging for the speedy transfer of her vast wealth.

In the fading light, Blake settles down onto the trailer's back steps and tears open the envelope. But before he can bring himself to begin reading the cursive on the pages within, he thinks, once again, that perhaps it's time to buy himself some folding chairs or maybe an outdoor chaise lounge of some kind—that maybe he really will stay here long enough to justify more than a trailer and the few sticks of furniture inside. And then he searches the property for any traces of Felix's ghost.

He knows they are with him always, and as if to remind him of this, they will often appear right at the edges of his vision even when he has not called them, bright-blue fireflies flickering in and out of visible life in the blink of an eye. He has driven his bike down many desert roads beneath vast, deep domes of stars, believing himself to be utterly alone, only to have them appear on all sides of him like excited dolphins chasing a ship. Rarely does the face of Felix Delachaise appear in their swirl or swarm, and usually only in those moments when Blake orders them into violent service in defense of someone who needs it. But they are always there, always at his service—a weapon and a shield. Without their omnipresence, he would never have the courage to ride a motorcycle at all, not after witnessing the terrible aftermaths of over a hundred motorcycle accidents during his years working in emergency rooms. If their recent behavior is any indicator, they are perfectly capable of catching him before the asphalt does.

Felix is capable, he corrects himself.

Blake summons them now, and they appear in a thickening, swirling column above the flowing creek, well out of sight of the road and the nearest neighbor thirty yards away. Their fierce blue light dapples the rushing, frothing water as the sun sinks deeper to the west and the edges of night begin their long trip across the dry valley floor. He can't face the past alone, not the sweet smell of Nova's perfume, not whatever request or news her letter might contain, and so he asks them to stay, luminous, swirling, and close, as he finally begins to read, and they obey his command without asking for a drop of his blood or a memory of his rage.

Dear Blake,

Daddy says I should give you your space, that you will come back in due time if that's what is meant to be. So I will have to ask his forgiveness, as well as yours, for tracking you down in this way. But please know that I have no intention of telling others where you're living. Along those lines, I ask you to destroy this letter as soon as you are finished reading it, as events here have forced . . . or maybe I should say allowed . . . us to return to lives that seem normal, at least on the surface. (That's why I wrote it by hand, BTW. So nobody could steal a piece of my history if they stole my computer.)

To be honest, I expected more of a fight from Caitlin's family, and it has saddened me in ways I never could have predicted to see how little love they have for her. I wonder, Blake, if you were perhaps the only person who ever truly loved her. But then I remember her parents and the attention they paid to her. It always seemed to me like love. But maybe that's just because it came wrapped in such glittering packages.

I think about her a lot, Blake. I think about her because I wonder how much of her was truly inside that . . . thing that came at me across the garden. There is a part of me that wants to know if a desire for my death was truly a part of her and if it came out in its purest form because she had been separated from her body. My father tells me these are foolish things to wonder about. He says the thing that Caitlin became was no thing at all, and so it doesn't matter. And maybe he's right.

What matters is that I never got a chance to thank you before you left. I saw what you did. I saw you make a choice, a choice that saved my life, and possibly my father's life and Allen's life and Sam's life. You could have hesitated. You could have tried to find out how much of Caitlin was still left, instead of saving my life the way you did. But you didn't, and for that, I will be in debt to you always.

I hope you decide to come back. There are things Daddy didn't see that night, things he doesn't understand, things you and I saw together, and so I will always feel connected to you, even though you have been changed (literally) by everything that happened and maybe that means you won't be able to live as normally (sort of) as we do. As we try to, I should say.

Spring House is mine now. I have a plan for it, but it is, in part, a plan that requires your approval. Here goes.

I would like to give part ownership of the house to the Lost Voices Project. I would like to put the slave quarters back and for there to be some sort of museum on the property, maybe something outside where the garden used to be. Something that shows the faces of the slaves who worked and died here. Something that shows all of history and not just the parts needed to rent the place out for weddings. But it doesn't feel right to invite people I care about, people like Dr. Taylor, onto this property without warning her in some way. And by warning her I mean giving her some kind of sense of what happened here that night . . . because it might happen again. I'm not sure that's a possibility, but I'm not sure it's not a possibility either.

Things have been quiet since you left, so maybe the secrets in the soil here are exhausted. But I worry. I worry about bringing others to this place, allowing them to give their hearts to it, if there's even the slightest chance that something like what we went through could happen again.

But our story is not mine alone to tell. I could always leave out the parts involving you, but still, it doesn't feel right not to say something to you first, not to ask your permission.

Write me, Blake. Please write me and tell me if I should proceed. Please write me and tell me that you're OK.

I trust that Felix Delachaise travels with you always, and I hope that he is truly under your command as you promised me he would be. If he is not, if you ever need help, you have a home at Spring House. You have a home with us always.

Your Friend,
Nova

PS, Speaking of miracles, we have taught Virginie how to read.

ACKNOWLEDGMENTS

Gwendolyn Hall, the scholar mentioned several times in this novel, is a real person, and I'm honored she took the time to correspond with me while I was researching this novel. The Lost Voices Project, however, is fiction. That said, if it were to exist, it would rely heavily on the work Ms. Hall did to compile an extensive database of one hundred thousand enslaved Africans and African Americans.

For invaluable and penetrating reads of *The Vines*, I'm indebted to David Groff and David Pomerico, as well as my own creative support system: my mother, Anne Rice, and my best friend and cohost of *The Dinner Party Show*, Eric Shaw Quinn.

The moment she read the manuscript, my agent, Lynn Nesbit, saw straight to the dark truth I tried to portray in this book. She also stuck with me during the various twists and turns on its exciting and sometimes suspenseful path toward publication.

I'm also blessed with excellent representation in the form of my attorney, Christine Cuddy, and my film and TV agent, Rich Green, at Resolution.

Along the way I received excellent counsel from my friends and colleagues Blake Crouch, Barry Eisler, Marcus Sakey, M.J. Rose, Liz Berry, and Gregg Hurwitz. (The always wise counsel of my best friend, Eric Shaw Quinn, is so pervasive throughout my life it almost doesn't rate a mention. But he likes attention, so I'll throw his name in one more time.) These fine folks all helped guide me toward new opportunities hiding amid new challenges.

The horror genre itself would still be a strange and forbidding world to me if it weren't for the excellent friendship and guidance of Michael Rowe, himself a very talented practitioner of scary, scary stories.

I'm smitten with the resourceful and incredibly smart team at 47North and Amazon Publishing. My thanks to Jason Kirk for spearheading the editorial process (and helping me come up with synonyms for the word *slut*, a word this novel was apparently full of when I first turned it in) and to Daphne Durham, Katie Finch, and Daniel Slater for introducing me to the exciting new world of Amazon Publishing.

When I published my last novel, *The Heavens Rise*, I left a very important person off of the acknowledgments page. Her name is Amy Loewy. She gave that novel a deep and thorough editorial read, and then I forgot to mention her. I bought her a nice dinner while I was in New Orleans, and I talked about her on Facebook a bunch, but still, I make it my business to give credit where credit is due. So thank you, Amy. Thanks to you and Britton for everything.

After two years, The Dinner Party Show, the Internet radio program I started with my cohost, Eric Shaw Quinn, has continued to be a joy and a challenge, and I'm grateful for the team that makes it happen every weekend. That team includes my cohost, Eric Shaw Quinn (again, of course), Brandon Griffith, Benjamin Scuglia, Jasun Mark, and Brett Churnin. Thanks, guys, for making sure Eric and I are even louder than usual every Sunday evening at 8:00 p.m. EST, 5:00 p.m. PST. (And the website, in case you ever want to listen, is www.thedinnerpartyshow.com.) And if you aren't one of our Party People, give us a listen (or a download) and see if we're your cup of tea. We have fun and we don't bite the first time you eat with us.

Do you love fiction with a supernatural twist?

Want the chance to hear news about your favourite authors (and the chance to win free books)?

Keri Arthur
Kristen Callihan
P.C. Cast
Christine Feehan
Jacquelyn Frank
Larissa Ione
Darynda Jones
Sherrilyn Kenyon
Jayne Ann Krentz and Jayne Castle
Lucy March
Martin Millar
Tim O'Rourke
Lindsey Piper
Christopher Rice
J.R. Ward
Laura Wright

Then visit the Piatkus website and blog
www.piatkus.co.uk | www.piatkusbooks.net

And follow us on Facebook and Twitter
www.facebook.com/piatkusfiction | www.twitter.com/piatkusbooks

piatkus